M000033191

LEGAL ENTERPRISE

by Janelle N. Nicholas

DayDreamers Publishing
www.daydreamerspublishing.com

DAYDREAMERS PUBLISHING

Cover design by Abrohn Creative
Interior design by Jessica Filippi

Library of Congress Cataloging-in-Publication Data applied for.
ISBN 978-0-9977119-0-5

ACKNOWLEDGEMENTS

To my wonderful family and friends, my mother, Linda Nicholas-Figueroa, my father Carl Nicholas, my step-mother, LaRhonda Nicholas, my sisters Angela and Kyndall Nicholas, my brother Donovan Nicholas, my nephew Marquel Bennet, and my niece Rylee Oliver and my brother-in-law, Darrell Oliver : this one is for you. I sincerely appreciate your comments, support, and suggestions.

Get ready for the second book in my Legal Enterprise series.

Please visit my website at www.daydreamerspublishing.com. You can also follow DayDreamers Publishing on Facebook at www. daydreamers.facebook.com\daydreamerspublishing and on Instagram at Daydreamerspublishing2016.

Peace and Love,

Janelle Nicholas
Baltimore, Maryland
February 2017

PROLOGUE

The sound of metal clanking rings in her ears. Janessa hears Agent Rodgers speak but she can't understand the words. As life fades from her coffee brown eyes, anger and betrayal consume her. Members of the bar, litigants, and judge's watch in shock and disbelief as she is escorted out of the Baltimore City courtroom in handcuffs. She makes the walk down the long, marble courtroom floors. Beady eyes peer at her. She keeps her head down and watches Agent Rodgers shiny black shoes for direction out the front door into the cool, fall morning

ONE

"You will arrive at your destination in 30 minutes; there are no traffic alerts now," the mechanical voice tells her. She arrives exactly 30 minutes later. Janessa pulls up to a tall, gray-brick building with broken windows. The sound of a train whistle filters through the air. Crows stare at her from the sills and ledges. She wonders if she's got the wrong address.

Her phone rings. She's not surprised when it's Vick. "Don't worry," he says, "you have the right place. Come on up to the third floor."

The thick, shiny, black door seems out of place on the entrance to this old, creepy building. When she tries the silver doorknob it's locked. A voice from a black box frightens her. "It should be open now." She tries again and it opens. Cold air rushes out, and Janessa must step back to gather herself together. She cautiously enters.

She treads softly, fearing the creaky floors will give way. She declines to take the humming, faded silver elevator, and climbs the stairs to the third floor. She locates the room. She's amazed to find herself in a room totally unlike the appearance of the outside of the building. The smell of lavender caresses her nose. There is a long black and brown conference table surrounded by several black chairs. Colorful digital fish dance along the wall in the 50-inch silver flat screen television. African-American paintings fill the other off-white walls. The blue and gold carpet looks imported. Soft music comes through a sound system. Janessa admires the décor. "Come on in," says Vick. Janessa enters slowly, then sits in one of the large comfortable black chairs. A short, African-American gentleman with bushy hair stands next to Vick.

"Let me introduce you to my man, Jarrod," Vick says.

Janessa shakes Jarrod's clammy wet hand. She resists the urge to wipe off her fingers on her jeans.

"Nice to meet you," she gives a half smile.

Jarrod nods.

"Relax. Everything is fine," claims Vick.

"I'm relaxed."

"No, you're not. I can see that from you face," he replies.

The wrinkles in her jaw subside as she unclenches her teeth.

"It's nice, huh?" Jarrod says.

"Yes, surprisingly," she answers.

"Yeah, my girl did the decorating. She swears she's the next Martha Stewart," laughs Jarrod.

"She did a nice job," says Janessa.

"Yeah, that's my girl," Jarrod replies.

"Okay, okay can we get down to business?" Vick interrupts.

He leans back in his chair, but just as he's about to speak, someone knocks on the door. Vick jerks his thumb toward his hip. He keeps his hand there as he booms: "Who is it?"

A voice from the other side speaks. "Yo, man, it's Te, chill!" Vick removes his hand from his hip.

"Come in."

A young man enters the room.

"What are you guys doing here?" he asks.

"This is my office. I can be here anytime I want to. What are you doing here?" Vick remarks.

"Came to drop off some stuff. I mean, should I come back some other time?" he says as he rubs his chin.

Vick turns to Jarrod.

"Hey man why don't you take him to the other spot to drop off the stuff."

"Okay man, catch ya later then," announces Jarrod. Te and Jarrod leave the room.

"Aright let's finally talk about what we came here for," boast Vick.

At that exact moment Malcolm Jacobs walks in, his expression hardened. Butterflies swarm Janessa's stomach. Malcolm doesn't acknowledge her. He gives Vick a gentleman's hug, and then sits at the head of the table. Malcolm is a few inches taller than Vick, and just as handsome. He has deep brown skin, a well-built body and a gleaming, white smile. His style is simpler than Vick's. Malcolm wears a pair of oversized dark blue sweat pants with a hoodie to match. He props a pair of fresh, white tennis shoes on the large conference table. In the few meetings Janessa has had with her client, she's never seen him dressed so casually.

"So it's been a while, attorney," says Malcolm.

Vick sits back, his face filled with devious satisfaction. She is speechless.

"Certainly not the greeting I was expecting," says Malcolm "Did she greet you like this?" he asks Vick.

"Naw, man, she was nothing but a lady with me," Vick says with a smirk.

"What's going on?" her voice quivers.

The men look at each other wondering which one should break the news. Malcolm speaks.

"We are here today because you are going to help us," he rubs his hands.

"Help you. Help you how?" she enquires.

"You're going to help us to help yourself," adds Vick.

"You're right, that would be a more accurate statement," states Malcolm.

The room spins; Janessa can barely breathe. Perspiration seeps from her pores.

"You okay?" Vick asks.

"I don't know." she replies.

"No need to feel nervous. I promise you this is going to be a win-win situation for all of us," says Malcolm.

"What's the win-win situation?" she questions.

Vick gets up and leaves, signaling that he'll be back. He returns with a brick shaped object wrapped in brown paper. He examines the object in the same way an appraiser would examine a piece of art.

"It's a beautiful thing, isn't it?" he inquires.

"How so?" Janessa wonders.

"Its purity, its simplicity and most importantly its worth!"

"It's worth?" she probes.

"Yes indeed. We're talking at least $10,000."

She reaches over and grabs the brick-shaped object with her sweaty palms from Vick's hands. It's lighter than she thought it would be.

"What does this have to do with me?" asks Janessa.

"I've been looking for someone like you to expand our business," admits Malcolm.

"What business?" she asks.

"The business of supplying people what they want—drugs, of course," Malcolm tells her.

Janessa's eyes pop open wide. She tries to say something, but no words come. Vick and Malcolm sit, waiting for her full reaction. She tries not to pass out.

Finally, she mutters: "Why me? And what am I supposed to do?" "Why you? You are the perfect front for the business," implores Vick.

"Why would you think that I would agree to something like this and not just turn you in to the authorities?" she demands.

Malcolm speaks up.

"Because you don't want to lose everything you've worked so hard for."

"That's nonsense," she responds angrily. "I would definitely lose everything by doing what you're asking me to do." Malcolm slams his hands on the table.

"And doing what you've been doing will bring success? I'm sure the Maryland Bar Commission and even the Baltimore City State's Attorney's Office wouldn't take kindly to learning that you've stolen tens of thousands of dollars from a client."

"I don't know what you're talking about," she responds, as the hairs on her arms begin to lift.

Malcolm's eyebrows furrow and his dark eyes fix onto Janessa. She notices the time on a digital display on the television. Though she feels like she's been there for hours, it's been less than thirty minutes.

"You know exactly what I'm talking about," barks Malcolm. "I can assure you that I'm the last person you want to play games with."

Her chin drops to her chest and she softly mutters: How long have you known?

"Excuse me, I didn't catch that." retorts Malcolm.

Janessa is unable to meet his eyes and continues to stare down at her chest.

"How long have you known?" she repeats herself.

"Since day one," responds Malcolm. "I have eyes and ears everywhere. Nothing gets past me, especially when it comes to my money."

"Why did you let it go on so long then?" asks Janessa.

"I was curious how far you would take it, how bold you could really be. That's where Vick came in. I had him keeping tabs on you. You know you're lucky that you're in such a unique position, otherwise … well, let's not make this an unpleasant moment. This is a time of celebration for all of us." He lifts his chin and smiles. She doesn't share his enthusiasm. Instead her throat thickens with sobs. Salty tears stream down her cheeks. The moment she's feared is here. Malcolm is either immune to her tears, or simply doesn't notice them. Vick at least hands Janessa a tissue.

"I swear it was only supposed to be one time. I don't know how it went out of control," she says in between tears and snuffles.

"I know exactly how it happened," snaps Malcolm. "You committed one of the seven deadly sins: greed."

"No," she cries. "It had nothing to do with greed; I didn't spend the money on luxuries. It was only to keep me afloat until business picked up. If you had just taken the plea deal three months ago, I would have never even considered doing something like this."

"Oh, so now it's my fault that you're an unethical attorney and a thief? Malcolm Jacobs should have taken a plea deal and gone to jail so Janessa Nikolas could save her business and live happily ever after," he went on as he clasps his large hands together.

It dawns on Janessa that what Malcolm has said is exactly what she'd meant. He's the bad guy anyway. It's his life that should be ruined by all his bad decisions, but instead it's her life falling apart because of one mistake after another.

"I didn't mean it that way," she says as she wipes away more tears.

"Sure you didn't," replies Malcolm.

"Let's just talk business already," interrupts Vick.

Vick pulls the brown paper-wrapped brick away from Janessa toward him. He takes out a small knife and runs the blade down the middle. White powder spills out from the brown paper. Malcolm and Vick regard it as treasure pulled from the depths. Janessa is too overwhelmed and exhausted to react.

Ring, ring …. Buzz, Buzz. Janessa and Vick both get calls at the

LEGAL ENTERPRISE

same instant. Vick gets up, and goes in a corner to answer. Janessa lets hers go to voicemail. Vick walks over to Malcolm and whispers something. Malcolm gives him a nod. Vick walks back over to the corner and resumes his phone conversation. He turns.

"Malcolm it's got to be now."

"Damn, aright. Tell him thirty minutes tops," replies Malcolm.

"Cool."

"I have to take care of something. Still reeling, huh?" Malcolm grins.

Janessa cast Malcolm a veiled glance.

"You fully expected to get away with it, didn't you? People like you always do," he sneers.

"Can I please leave?" she pleads.

"Of course. You were always free to leave. Ain't nobody keeping you hostage. You chose to stay because ... well honestly, you didn't have much of a choice." Malcolm laughs.

"We'll be in touch real soon," he tells her.

"Hey man, we got to leave if we're going to make it on time," Vick stresses.

"Aright." Malcolm walks over to Janessa and reaches to shake her hand.

Janessa extends her sweaty palm, weakly returning the shake.

"I know you can do better than that," Malcolm says, "but I'll give you a pass for today."

Malcolm leaves. Janessa doesn't move. She's frozen. Vick tries to reassure her with a pat on the shoulder.

"Look, I know it's a lot to take in, but it's not as bad as you think. Trust me, this will work, and you will be successful—exactly what you want, right?"

She doesn't answer. Instead she concentrates on getting up and walking out. Vick accompanies her. Malcolm is nowhere to be found. Vick starts toward the fading silver elevator. Janessa hesitates.

-9-

"What's wrong? You don't like elevators?"

"No, I don't like elevators that don't appear to work," she says

"Come on. I would never put the key to our fortune in harm's way." He motions for her to get on. She folds her arms.

"I'll just go back the way I came, thanks."

"Fine. I'll meet you downstairs."

Janessa hurries down the shallow, black steps. Vick is waiting at the bottom and they exit the building together. He opens her car door. "After you, madam." "Sure," she says.

Hot air trickles through her cracked car window as she drives home. She recalls her decision to take unearned funds from her escrow account. She knew it was a big risk as taking unearned funds from escrow was one of the easiest and quickest ways to get disbarred and even possibly be charged with a crime. The first time she took money she was so nervous; she threw up twice before reaching the bank. Lost in the memory, she passes her apartment and goes two more blocks before she realizes it. She swings into an empty parking lot and turns off her radio. Despite the warm night, she is shaking all over. Her phone rings— it's her best friend Gina. Janessa doesn't have the energy to fake a positive attitude, so she lets the call go to voicemail.

She drives back to her apartment and finds street parking directly in front. Her eyelids close. She's startled awake by banging on the driver's side window. It's one of her neighbors. She rolls down her window.

"Hello, are you okay?"

"Hey I'm fine. I guess I was so tired I fell asleep right in the car."

"Okay, I was just checking on ya. Thought you was dead for a second." He teases.

As she laughs with him, she wonders if being dead would be a better alternative. "Thanks for checking on me," she utters. "I'm going inside now, and take my ass to bed."

"Good idea," he says, then he walks away. Janessa swings open her car door. Her attempt to get out of the car fails. Exhaustion pulls her back into the car seat. As her eyes start to close again, the blaring sirens of a Baltimore City fire truck scare her. She wills herself out of the car and goes into her apartment. Truth and Justice welcome her. The instinctual four-legged mammals know that something is wrong and they begin to whimper. Her eyes are glossy, tears stream down her face onto her pink t-shirt. She struggles for breath, and tries to calm herself. That's not easy. Janessa is now realizing her life is forever changed.

TWO

Janessa sits in the middle of the floor of her tiny bathroom. As tears run down her face, she hears her phone ringing. She can't recall where she left it. Unable to speak to anyone, she remains seated on the bathroom floor. With her head in her hands she goes over the meeting with Vick and Malcolm. When she finally manages to exit the bathroom, the apartment is unnervingly quiet. Truth and Justice sit by the door waiting. Janessa pets her dogs reassuringly. The pain of dragging herself into bed makes her want to scream: "Why me?" But she doesn't have the energy. Her eyes are puffy from crying. All her body has the energy to do is to lie lifelessly on her bed. Janessa is jumpy and jittery all night and gets no sleep. All she can think about is Malcolm's "offer" to work for him or he reports her to the Maryland Bar and the Baltimore City State's Attorney's Office. She ponders if she were to turn herself in first if she would be spared any repercussions. However, the thought of her family and friends knowing what she did and that she was not the success they thought she was, frightens her just as much as Malcolm's offer, if not more.

By the time an early phone call from her sister, Angel comes in, Janessa has still not made her decision. Angel is calling to ask if she could drop off Janessa's nephew and niece, Marquel and Rylee, so she can take a last-minute hair client. Janessa is in no shape to take on the quasi parent role and declines. Although frustrated, Angel agrees to ask another family member. Janessa apologizes to her sister and hangs up. She tries to get some sleep when she realizes she missed a call from Malcolm. Her hands shake and her heart pounds as she calls him back. Malcolm answers the phone right away.

"How are you feeling?" he says as soon as he answers the phone.

"I've been better," she relates.

"Everything will be fine. You'll see," he insists.

"What's next?" she asks.

"Meet me at the same place this evening around 8pm and I'll tell you."

"Fine." Janessa hangs up the phone.

For the first time since yesterday morning she looks at herself in her full-length mirror. Her red-rimmed eyes are a scary sight. She attempts to run her hand through her matted hair. Her face is stained with the salt residue of her tears. She puts on a baseball cap, flip-flops, and a pair of oversized black sweatpants left by an old boyfriend. She takes a long walk with Truth and Justice.

Despite what happened yesterday, she is still Malcolm's attorney. Nonetheless, she cannot bring herself to do any work. Her only thoughts are about being in that room with Malcolm and Vick and the events that led her there. She'd always thought she would only have to do it once. Never did she anticipate a second time, then a third and a fourth. Blaming Malcolm is fruitless, because she knows the responsibility is her own. "Would've," "could've," and "should've" bounce around in her head like ping-pong balls. She tries to distract herself by looking for something to wear to that night's meeting. After pulling several items from the closet she finally decides. When she sees it's only 4:30 she wishes time would hurry up. Janessa doesn't know what to do with herself. She tries to lie down, but it's a lost cause. Around 5:30 she gets on the Internet to do some research on her blackmailers. First, a Google search of Vick's name, along with Malcolm's. She finds Vick mentioned in several articles. One catches her attention.

It's a five-year-old newspaper article about corrupt cops working with drug dealers. Vick was one of several cops under investigation. Janessa tries to read the whole article, but the link to the article is not working. Oddly, no other mentions of the investigation, or other related links can be found.

The clock now reads 6:30. "Wow 6:30 already," she says. Too nervous to wait any longer, she starts getting ready. As Janessa adds on her favorite charm bracelet, she stares at the multiple trinkets dangling from her arm: Steelers charm, heart charm, dog charm, and the rest. This gift from an ex-boyfriend reminds her of a simpler, happier time. Pushing those thoughts from her mind, she completes her preparations with a touch of perfume on her neck.

Reentering the spooky gray building at exactly 8pm gives her the chills. When she arrives back in the elaborate conference room, she notices new paintings on the wall. The previous day's soft music plays through the ceiling speakers. Malcolm sits at the head of the table. Janessa sits a couple chairs down from him, and waits.

Malcolm doesn't say anything. He gets up, and leaves Janessa alone in the room for about ten minutes. She toys with a lock of her hair, and bounces her left leg up and down. Malcolm returns, carrying a large army green duffel bag. He sets it down in the middle of the table and sits back down.

"Here it is," informs Malcolm, "everything you need to start your practice."

"Start my practice? My practice is already up and running," she replies.

"My apologies. It's everything you need to start OUR practice. Aren't you even going to look in the bag?"

She rises and hesitantly pulls the bag closer so she can open it.

Unzipping the bag, she finds bundles of green paper stacked on top of each other.

"What's this for?"

"I just told you, everything you need to start our practice." Janessa sits back down and puts her head in her left hand.

"What am I supposed to do with all this money?"

"The setup you have now isn't suitable for our clients. When they walk into our office they'll expect to see something like this." He motions to their current surroundings. "We have a much better space for you to use, fully furnished."

"So what do I need the money for?" she inquires again.

"Décor, computers, I don't know: lawyer stuff. How about a little gratitude? I just threw $5,000 at you to spend as you please."

"I can't be grateful for this," she whimpers.

"I think you need to come off your high and mighty cloud," he lectures. "You do understand you brought this on yourself?"

"I do," Janessa says turning away.

"Let me ask you something: why? You seem like such a good girl. Always following the rules and shit."

"I thought it would be no problem for me to start my own practice right out of law school," she narrates. "Everyone around me figured I would be an instant success. When I realized failure was imminent I panicked."

"So failure isn't an option for you, huh?" suggests Malcolm.

"It didn't used to be an option. I am certainly learning that failure is not the same as defeat," she says.

"You know, you don't have to do this," he declares, bringing a brief light to her face.

"But if you don't I will have no choice but to report you to the Bar, and, of course, the prosecutor's office."

Her hopes dim. She looks up at the ceiling, as if waiting for a sign from the heavens, but none appears. She must make the decision herself.

"You haven't really given me much of a choice," she emphasizes.

"It's a choice. Either work for Vick and I , or be disbarred, and possibly go to a jail or have a criminal record at the least." He takes too much pleasure in the words.

Malcolm is right, she does have a choice, but if she wants to stay out of jail and not be a disgrace to her family, she doesn't.

"When do we start?" she mutters.

"ASAP. We should have been making money as of yesterday. So, you ready for this? Because once you're in, there's no turning back."

"I'm as ready as any person could be for this kind of situation."

Malcolm comes over to her side of the table. She stands up. The smell of peppermint penetrates her nose as he looks down at her.

He reaches out, and they shake.

"Welcome to the jungle," he declares.

THREE

It's the evening of the open house for her new practice. The décor of the firm is top of the line. Brown leather chairs adorn the lobby. The conference room table shines, and so do the black leather chairs circling it. The floors of the office are covered with power red carpeting. The library looks like something out of the movies and the walls are lined from top to bottom with books. There are many people there: her parents, sisters, brother, nephew, niece, cousins, close friends, former co-workers and even former employers. Everyone is impressed with her new office, making her feel empowered. People are enjoying themselves with catered delectables, good wine, and sodas for those who aren't drinking alcohol.

Suddenly – Bang! Bang! Bang! Without warning several heavily armed men in black storm the room!

"FBI, FBI everybody get on the floor!"

Janessa tries to tell the FBI agents that it's her they want. She asks if they could please let everyone else go. They answer with a threat of force, telling her to shut up and lie down. The fear in her mother and little sister's faces pierces her soul. She tries to mouth the words "I'm sorry" to them, but she can't get her lips to move.

BOOM! Janessa jumps up from her bed.

"Oh my God, it was just a nightmare," she stammers. Her sweat-soaked shirt hangs from her body, her heart thudded and her stomach knotted. Thunder booms, and the familiar sound of rain resonates through her bedroom. Janessa drags herself into the bathroom, where she splashes cold water on her face. With her thoughts of the nightmare lingering she can't fall back to sleep. Soon night turns to day. When the first rays of sun hit her window, she starts pacing.

It's only 7a.m., so she climbs back in bed and tries to get more sleep. As soon as her head hits the pillow her phone rings. It's an unknown number and she's too tired to talk. The ringing stops, then starts up again a minute later: the same unknown number. Though she still doesn't answer, she decides it's time to get up. After a few rounds of yawning and stretching she finally rises from her foam mattress. She dreads her task for the day.

Malcolm has given Janessa instructions about meeting his "guy" at the bank. He tells her she must be there promptly at 10am. His guy will set her up with a business bank account. By the time she meets with Malcolm's guy, he will have the $5,000. He'll set it up to look like the money is a business loan she received from the bank, then he will start a business account from which she can withdraw funds. Malcolm has told her that his guy will recognize her. He described the guy as clean-cut, white, with short dirty blond hair. She leaves her apartment and heads to the bank. When she arrives, she's greeted by a sunburned male around 30, with sandy blond hair, and wearing a two- piece brown suit.

"Hi, can I help you today?" he raises his hand in greeting.

"Yes, I'm here to set up a business account," she responds.

"No problem, I will gladly help you with that. Just follow me to my office."

Janessa follows him to an office bordered by glass walls. Once she sits down, he closes the door and locks it.

As he sits down behind a black flat screen computer, he says:

"Nice to meet you Janessa. As you probably already know, my name is Steve."

"No, I didn't know, but nice to meet you, Steve."

"Okay, so you say you need a business account, right."

"Oh, umm, yes, that's right. I need to set up a business account for my law practice," Janessa responds almost in the form of a question.

"Great, let me get you set up then," he remarks.

He starts tapping away on his computer. He asks her for two forms of identification. She gives him her driver's license and social security card. She is curious as to why someone like Steve is willing to help Malcolm. Steve looks like an average working man who probably goes home every night to his wife and children. She observes a silver wedding band on his ring finger, but his desk has no family photos. He also wears a silver watch with small diamonds lining the face. His heavy cologne tickles Janessa's nose and the walls display several framed degrees, but none of them from local schools. The two remain quiet with only the click clack of Steve's typing to break the silence.

The click clack finally stops. Steve rises from his seat and leaves the office. A minute later he reappears with some starter checks and a temporary bankcard. He gives them to her, explaining that she can use them for anything she wants: printers, computers, fax machines, even clothing; whatever she feels she needs to start the practice. He also instructs her to keep an accurate account of everything she spends for Malcolm and Vick's review.

"Is that all?" she questions.

"That's it. You're all set. I look forward to doing business with you."

"Right," she mutters.

When she leaves the bank, she stands still and closes her eyes, hoping that when she opens them everything will be back to the way it was before she met Malcolm. Even with her eyes closed she can feel the presence of pedestrians walking around her. One part of her wants to go back in the bank while she still can. She could return the checkbook and bankcard and run for her life. But she feels she has no choice. Taking this money seems like her only chance to save whatever dignity she has left.

By the time she pulls into Office Depot's parking lot the temperature is ninety degrees. She strips off a couple of layers of clothing before leaving the car. Never in her short life has she ever walked into a store—not even a dollar store-- without worrying about how much she could spend. She buys a printer, laptop, computer paper, paper, pencils, ink, computer desk, chair, and has new business cards made. She wishes she could enjoy this experience, but she feels like a slave following her masters' orders. The whole experience makes her crumble inside and she's relieved when it's over. She barely gets a foot in the door when her phone starts ringing.

"Yes?" she answers.

"I would have expected a warmer welcome once you've spent my money," growls Malcolm, "but that's alright. This isn't anything new to you."

"I bought everything you asked me to," she responds.

"Good. I'll text you the address of your new office and you can set up tomorrow."

"Fine."

"Hey, don't sound too excited."

"It's been a long day," she says.

"You'll show your appreciation soon enough," Malcolm remarks.

"Of course I'm appreciative," she says in a hollow voice.

"I'll be by the office around noon. Be there."

The line abruptly goes dead. She mopes as she trudges upstairs to her bedroom, the dogs following behind her. She's cried so much in the last couple days; she has no more tears left. She drops to her knees at the edge of her bed, and begins to pray. She doesn't pray out loud. Instead she silently speaks to God, until she feels Justice's warm, moist tongue on her cheek, and she ends her prayer.

As she lifts herself off the ground she groans in pain. Though it's not very late, she strips down to her underwear, throws on an old gym t-shirt, and goes downstairs to relax on the couch. The warmth of her favorite fleece Steelers blanket soothes her as she aimlessly watches television. As night falls, she slips in and out of sleep. Each time her eyes close she has a nightmare. Her nightmares are so vivid, that she loses all sense of reality.

Two hours later she finally gives up and hobbles to the kitchen. She passes a sink full of dirty dishes and makes her way to the refrigerator. When she opens her refrigerator door the rush of cold air feels amazing. She has no idea why she's looking in here. A half-gallon of lactose-free milk is all she has. Goose bumps form on her arms, prompting her to close the sad, empty fridge. She hopes that the sun never rises. Then she wouldn't have to go to the office. She sees the new office as a prison. Her own mistakes are the bars, Vick is her guard, and Malcolm is the warden.

Her prayers fail to stop the sunrise. She wakes on her living room couch to chirping birds. She hears the familiar sound of her alarm clock coming from upstairs. Even though this is "the day" unexpectedly she doesn't feel nervous. No butterflies, no nausea, no anxiety. She pinches her brown skin to make sure she's awake. She squeezes the flesh so hard that she leaves behind visible marks. "Ouch" she says. She is awake, yet she still feels a sense of calm. She glides upstairs to her room and turns off her alarm. She pulls a black skirt suit from her closet. It has thin white stripes and a white button up blouse with ruffles around the collar. It's the perfect combination. She even pulls out her costume pearl necklace and matching earrings.

Vick calls as she is putting her makeup on. "So you ready for your big day?" he asks.

"As ready as I can be," she says.

"Fine. Well, have a good one," he responds.

He hangs up. As she hears the empty dial tone her nerves kick in. She knows the moment she enters that office; she can't escape what she is about to do.

FOUR

Janessa rubs her hands up and down her skirt as she drives. Her friend, Gina, calls again to check in on her. Janessa claims to be doing great. She even tells Gina about her "new" office space. Another façade, Janessa thinks to herself. Her family and friends believe she's successful when the reality is quite different.

She has her sister, Angel, meet her at the new office. They spend two hours putting things together. Shortly after they finish, Angel leaves. She has plenty to do at her own business, a hair salon called Element Beauty Studio in Glen Burnie that she co-owned with their cousin, Shauna. Standing alone in the middle of the office, Janessa can't help but admire it. The huge desk is of a modern glass design. She has a tall, red leather chair, which she finds interesting. Two other smaller red chairs will seat potential clients. The rug underneath her desk is black and white with an abstract print. Her sister has added a decorative flare with a couple of flower arrangements, paintings and a few family pictures. These make the office feel homier. Suddenly she recognizes that this office is a lot like the one in her nightmare, chills run down her spine.

She isn't sure what she should be doing, so for the next hour she twiddles her thumbs and plays on her smart phone. When her office phone rings, she answers. A young man on the other end asks her if she is available. When she says yes, he tells her he needs to meet with her right away. Confused but interested, Janessa gives him the address and hangs up the phone. The young man arrives about 45 minutes later. He's clean cut, wears purposefully ripped jeans, and a white, gray and purple-striped shirt.

His hands are jammed in his pockets. She sits him down, and pours him a glass of water.

"My name is Zack," he announces.

"Okay, Zack, what can I do for you?"

"I got myself into a little trouble last night while I was hanging out in the city with some friends," he says, then he goes silent.

"Okay, you'll have to elaborate a little more for me. I promise, even if you decide not to hire me, anything you tell me will remain confidential."

"Okay, well, me and some friends got caught smoking weed last night."

"Where?"

"At some girl's house in Mt. Vernon. There were six of us chilling, smoking and drinking, when suddenly police are handcuffing us, and ripping up the house."

"Did they arrest you?" ponders Janessa.

"No they didn't, they didn't arrest anybody ... it was the weirdest thing," exclaims Zack.

"So let me understand this, they burst into the house, and then do nothing?"

He shakes his head.

"No. They tore the place apart like they were looking for something specific."

"And then what?"

"Nothing. They left." Noting the skeptical look on Janessa's face, he adds: "I swear that's what happened."

"I'm not saying it didn't happen Zack, but it doesn't make

much sense. Maybe you're missing some details because you were scared, high and drunk."

"Maybe."

"Besides if they didn't arrest you, what do you need me for?"

"I don't know. I just figured that I needed a lawyer," he reasons. "I understand why you would think that, but honestly there's not much I can do for you right now."

She is about to hand Zack a card when she remembers he called her office, implying he already had her information.

"By the way. How did you come to call my office?" she questions. "What do you mean? You're a lawyer, right?"

"Yes, but there are at least 100 other lawyers you could have called in the city alone. How did you come to call me?" she repeats.

"Look I have to go. Thanks for the advice though."

Zack hurries out of Janessa's office. Janessa wonders if the story he told had any truth to it and why he was so evasive about her question. She starts to play on her smart phone again when another call comes in on the office phone. She answers. It's her sister Angel.

"Any new clients yet?"

"Someone did come to the office," says Janessa.

"They decided not to hire you?" asks Angel.

"Not now."

They chat for a few more minutes about the kids and business in general. Janessa decides to have an early lunch and goes across the street to a sandwich shop. After she finishes lunch, she sits at her desk for about an hour. No calls come in. Out of boredom she starts to text random people and see how their days are going. She doesn't get any responses, and knows they must be busy—unlike her. She is about to try more texts when her office door flings open. Janessa looks up, her forehead creases when she realizes that it's Vick.

"Aw, you don't look happy to see me," he grins.

"No, it's not that. I'm a little annoyed that I've been sitting here all day doing nothing."

"I understand," says Vick. "When I first got out of the Academy I was anxious to get out there on the streets and arrest some bad guys right away."

"You're a police officer?" Janessa asks.

"Detective," he corrects her.

"Sorry," she mumbles.

"Former detective to be more accurate."

"Why are you working for the other side now?"

"That's a long story, too long. But one of these days I'll tell you."

"Well can I at least get the beginning?" asks Janessa.

"I guess I can tell you a little something."

She gets comfortable in her chair, like a child getting ready for story time.

"I was born and raised in the City of Baltimore . I'd wanted to be a cop ever since I could remember."

"Was your dad a cop?" Janessa chimes.

"No, I didn't know my father."

Before he can continue Zack comes in. Vick greets him first.

"Hey man, what's up?" says Vick.

Janessa's head flinches back slightly and she sits quietly.

"Nice to see you again," Zack says to Janessa.

"What's going on?" she demands.

"You passed the test," Vick replies.

"The test?"

"Yes, Malcolm and I wanted to be sure that you wouldn't jump the gun and say or do something you shouldn't have."

She folds her arms, and frowns like a disgruntled child.

"Hey, don't take it personally," asserts Vick. He looks at Zack.

"Hey man, give us a minute."

"No problem." Zack leaves the room.

"Was a test really necessary?" asks Janessa, once Zack is gone.

"Absolutely," Vick responds.

"So what exactly were you testing?"

"Well for starters we wanted to be sure that you weren't going to offer drugs to any Tom, Dick or Harry who walks in." Janessa rolls her eyes, but calms down. Vick calls for Zack to come back in.

"Thanks for your help today," Vick says to him, then he pulls a roll of money from his jacket's breast pocket, peels off a few bills, and hands them to Zack. Janessa can't tell what denomination they are, but based on Vick's style she assumes they're either hundreds or fifties.

"Anytime," states Zack.

He waves bye to Janessa and leaves the office.

"So now what?" she requests.

"First let me show you where you'll be keeping the stuff," says Vick.

"Where's Malcolm?" asks Janessa.

"He had to take care of something. He should be here tomorrow," Vick replies.

He eases past Janessa's red office chair, and pushes a painting aside. Behind the painting is a keypad. As Vick pushes buttons, they glow blue, and a section of the light green wall starts to move.

"This is where we'll keep everything," he instructs.

"It doesn't look very big," she murmurs.

"It's large enough to hold 50 pounds of product easily. It can also fit two or three adults if necessary." "So do I get your code?" she interjects.

"Nope," he responds.

"How am I supposed to put anything in it or get anything out?"

"Everybody has their own code. That way we can keep tabs on when you are in the safe, and for how long."

"Okay, so when do I get my own code?"

"In time."

"You don't trust me?"

"No, that's not it. You don't need it right now. You'll learn that a lot of this business is on a need-to-know basis. When you need to know something, you will."

"Okay, fine," she says.

"So how much longer did you plan on hanging out here?" Vick asks.

"I don't know. It's 5 o'clock. I guess I can call it a day."

"You should. It won't be long before you're wishing you could leave work this early."

"How late are we talking?" she scoffs.

"We'll go into that some other time. I promise you, when the money starts rolling in, it will be more than worth it," stresses Vick.

Janessa sighs, and she looks at herself in the mirror on her phone. Her once bright eyes have a haunted look. Vick walks her to her car. She tells Vick goodnight and heads home. Loud music booms through her car speaker. The thumping of her heart is so powerful; she can hear it over the songs. Her legs feel like heavy weights as she treks up the steps to her bedroom.

Getting out of the bed the next morning is taxing. She slips on a purple dress. Her phone rings. "What now Vick?" she says to herself out loud. As she reaches for the phone it drops on the floor and the battery shoots out like a bullet from a gun. Janessa falls back onto the bed, closes her eyes, takes a deep breath, and gets back up. She picks up the phone. After placing the battery in the phone, she turns it back on. The missed call wasn't Vick; it was her mom. She decides to call her back later, and scurries out of her apartment.

At the office, a young Asian woman is waiting. She's petite, with jet-black hair that falls to her shoulders. Her black suit looks top of-the-line, and she wears a pink blouse to accent it. Startled by the woman's presence, Janessa doesn't speak right away. The woman doesn't speak either, which seems a little peculiar.

They stand, staring at each other, until the woman finally speaks up: "Um, h-h-hi are you Janessa?"

"Yes, I am. How can I help you?"

"I was told to come see you."

"Okay, see me about what?"

The woman is quiet again. She looks down at the floor and fidgets with the sleeve of her suit jacket.

"I was told you would know why I'm here."

Janessa believes this is another test from Vick and Malcolm. She remembers that she's never supposed to serve anyone claiming to have been sent by one of them. Janessa is hesitant to say anything.

Again, the two women stare at each other in awkward silence.

"I'm sorry, there must have been some kind of miscommunication. I don't know what you're talking about," stammers Janessa.

The woman's lips curl and her nostrils flare. She leaves. Janessa instantly calls Vick.

"There was a woman here. But she left."

"Damn. I'll be there in a few minutes."

The phone goes dead. Vick arrives at the office twenty minutes later.

"Your client will be back in about ten minutes." Vick hands Janessa a very small sliver of paper, which she instinctively throws in the trashcan.

"Hey, hey what are you doing?" asks Vick.

"Oh, I thought you wanted me to throw this away," she contests.

"No, I can throw my own trash away. If I ever hand you something it's for you to look at," states Vick.

"Sorry about that."

"It's cool. The best lessons are learned through experience," he smiles.

She unwraps the sliver of paper and sees a six-digit number.

She and Vick go to the wall safe, where she carefully pushes each soft button. Blue lights glow behind each button, captivating her. The buttons don't make a sound, but in her head Janessa hears a beep with each touch. When the safe door opens, Vick walks in and pulls out a large prescription bottle containing a couple hundred pills. Within seconds of removing the bottle from the safe, the Asian woman returns. Vick takes a chair a few feet from Janessa. Janessa apologizes to the woman for the earlier confusion, and asks her to please be seated. The woman sits. She seems much more comfortable with Vick there.

"How can I help you?" asks Janessa.

"I need fifty," says the woman.

Janessa opens the bottle and counts out fifty of the small white pills in increments of ten. The woman pulls out her own prescription bottle from her purse and hands it to Janessa. She is surprised, but plays it cool and follows along. She fills the bottle with the fifty pills, and hands it back to the woman. Before Janessa can read the name on the bottle the woman snatches it back. The woman then hands her two crisp one-hundred-dollar bills. Janessa looks over at Vick, not sure if this is the exact price. Vick nods in approval, and she puts the cash in her desk. The woman gets up and departs the office. Janessa's chest is tight. She realizes she is holding her breath and lets out a big gasp of air.

"How do you feel?" asks Vick.

"I'm not sure."

"Well you did fine."

"It would have been nice to know how much she is supposed to pay."

"Oh they all know that only exact amounts are accepted here. We don't give change." "Two hundred dollars for fifty pills. That's an expensive habit," declares Janessa.

"True, but expensive for them means rich for us, right?" he replies.

"She looked so normal. What's her story?"

"Professional woman, mother and wife who found herself addicted to oxycodone. That's all," he says.

"Is that something you see a lot of?"

"I see a lot of everything, and soon so will you! Let's take a tour of the safe."

Janessa walks over to the safe and puts in her code. She looks inside and she can see pill bottles filled with blue, white, and yellow pills. Some are large, others small. She also notices what looks like small bundles of marijuana. She turns to Vick.

"Just pills and marijuana?"

"Oh excuse me, what else should we have?"

"I guess I figured we would be selling what you showed me in the conference room that day." she advises.

"Man, you're ready for the big stuff now , huh?" Vick chuckles.

"I'm not ready for any of this. I was thinking the more money, and the faster we make it, the sooner I can get out of this."

"We are not even one week in and you're already talking about getting out!"

"Yes. The sooner the better." Janessa urges.

After a couple of hours Malcolm arrives. His dark gray slacks fit him perfectly. His watch is plain, but large, and very gold.

"You got a nice set up here," he says. "I was hoping we could make good use of this space."

Janessa's skin flushes when Malcolm grins at her. Vick is watchful. She feels a strange glow from the attention both men give her. Malcolm pushes buttons on the safe. His buttons light up green, not blue.

"Where's the rest?" Malcolm roars to Vick

"At the other location. She's not ready for that," responds Vick

"You're not ready for the big stuff, huh?" Malcolm taunts Janessa.

"Vick says I'm not," replies Janessa meekly.

"Yeah, but what do YOU think?" asks Malcolm.

"If I start with the hard stuff, will it help me get from under this faster?" she responds.

"Possibly. The more money, and the faster we make it, the

better," Malcolm implies. He turns toward Vick.

"I say she's ready."

Vick gives Malcolm a glassy stare.

"Okay, it's your call. I can bring the stuff over later tonight, if that's what you want." informs Vick.

"Yeah, that's what I want," reiterates Malcolm.

Vick and Malcolm discuss the logistics while Janessa listens. Vick tells Janessa she will need to be there when they go to get the stuff. She turns to Malcolm, and asks if he will be there too.

"Of course, this is my business," he says.

"Fine, we'll all be there," says Vick, carefully controlling his voice and tone.

"Naw, man, you don't need to be there. Janessa and I can handle it," declares Malcolm.

"What you mean?" asks Vick.

"Exactly what I said, we can handle it. Go home to your girl tonight, relax a little," says Malcolm.

She slips Vick a curious glance at Malcolm's mention of his girl. Is this "girl" a girlfriend? Wife? Maybe a daughter? Janessa ponders to herself. Either way, she's startled Vick has failed to mention either one.

"Man, I think I should be there," Vick protests. "I've been holding this thing down for all the years you were gone. Now I'm just supposed to leave everything to you and her?"

"You knew from the beginning who ran this. Don't act surprised now!" Malcolm warns.

Vick suggests that they step outside to continue the conversation. The two excuse themselves and leave. Janessa's adrenaline runs high and she decides to stick around. She feels like she's in a movie. Minutes later they return.

"You're going to go with Vick to the spot to get the stuff, okay," says Malcolm

Soon after Malcolm and Vick leave the office. Janessa stays, and wonders what happened to change Malcolm's mind. She does an Internet search on Malcolm, reading numerous articles on his federal conviction for drug distribution and weapons possession. One article speaks about a thirty-year sentence, but he got out after eighteen on a technicality. She wonders if these two men have families. Neither has spoken of relatives. Malcolm's mention of Vick's "girl" was the first, and only indication of anyone special in either man's life. That night neither man calls on Janessa to pick up the "stuff". Three weeks pass without any mention of it. During most of the summer Janessa trains for her new role as drug supplier to the professionals of Baltimore City. As Vick and Malcolm constantly press her about the need to make more money, she catches on quickly. Before she can blink fall leaves are swirling outside her office window. The guilt and shame eventually fade, as she grows accustomed to being Malcolm and Vick's puppet.

FIVE

One night, ringing scares Janessa right out of her bed, giving her an instant headache. It takes a few seconds before she realizes her cell phone is ringing. When she answers, Vick is on the other end. He's finally available to go get the stuff. Janessa is trying to gather herself. She looks at the time: 2a.m.

"Can't this wait?" she asks.

"I know you are sleeping, but in this business things got to be done when they can be done," says Vick.

"Are you going to pick me up?" she asks.

"Yes, I'll be there in thirty minutes. Throw something on. If all goes well, we should be done in an hour at most."

"Okay, see you in thirty minutes then."

"Cool."

Janessa's dogs are up too, and they want to go outside. "Might as well," she says to herself. Janessa throws on her favorite all-purpose black sweatpants, and the blouse she wore to work. She also puts on some flip-flops. It only takes her five minutes to get ready, and that's evident by what a hot mess she looks. She takes Truth and Justice out, and by the time she gets back, Vick has sent a text stating he's around the corner. She steps back outside just in time to see a shiny black luxury SUV pull up.

It stops in front of Janessa. The menacing tinted windows make her hesitate before opening the door. The SUV doesn't budge and she waits for some kind of indication that this is Vick. The window slowly rolls down and she sees Vick's white teeth peeking out from the darkness.

"Are you waiting for the red carpet to roll out?" Vick asks.

"No, but how am I supposed to know it's you with those pitch-black windows!"

"I did just text you and say I was around the corner," he says, giving Janessa a once-over.

"Man, when I said throw something on you sure did take that literally."

Janessa blushes with embarrassment and climbs in the truck.

"Yeah, I did."

"That's cool. Lucky for you nobody will see you dressed so crazy," he says, and they drive off.

"So, just me and you?" she asks.

"Yep. Is that okay with you?"

"Yeah. Malcolm runs things around here?" she says, making it half-question and half-statement.

Vick's furrows his brow, and he rakes his hand through his hair. He doesn't reply.

"How long have you and Malcolm known each other?" Janessa asks Vick, as they pull into the winding driveway of a small, white, country-style home.

"Enough of the personal stuff," he says. "Let's take care of this business so we can both get home and get some sleep."

As Janessa opens her door, Vick adds: "Oh, you don't need to come in. I'll only be a few minutes. It will be quicker that way."

Janessa is happy to stay in the truck and relax while Vick goes into the house. She adjusts the soft, heated seat, and closes her eyes. Bright porch lights penetrate her closed eyelids. Her eyes have been closed for about fifteen minutes when Vick opens the back of the SUV. She doesn't open her eyes but she can hear him grunting and moaning as he puts something in the back. She hears the back close, and Vick gets into the driver's seat.

"Come on, wake up. One more stop then back home to your bed," states Vick.

"I'm awake. I'm just resting my eyes."

"Aright, we'll be there in a few minutes and when we do you'll need to get out."

"Okay."

They arrive at the law office. Janessa slowly opens her eyes. She stretches her arms, and rolls her neck.

"Okay, sleeping beauty. Let's get to work," pronounces Vick.

She walks around to the back of the truck where Vick is already unloading a bulky black gym bag.

"How can I help?" she inquires.

"I got the bag. Just open the door for me."

"No problem."

She uses her key to open the front door of the office. They go in together, and Vick heads for the safe, with Janessa following behind.

"Man, that's heavy," he grunts.

She struggles to stay engaged, and doesn't respond to Vick's comment.

"I know you're tired. I'm going to get you home," says Vick.

Janessa can't figure out why she had to come anyway. She didn't do anything. When Vick opens the bag, Janessa sees square blocks wrapped in brown paper. He unloads ten of them into the safe. Janessa assumes it's cocaine, but she's too tired to ask questions. Vick doesn't explain anything. He finishes, closes the safe, and tells Janessa to get back in the truck. She gladly complies, looking forward to returning to bed. They head back to her house. He tells her that he knows she's tired, and that she doesn't need to open the office until 10:30 tomorrow. Janessa is grateful.

By the time they reach her apartment, her eyes are closed again. She hears R&B music playing in the background. Unexpectedly, someone's lips touch hers. Instead of opening her eyes, she remains limp, pretending she doesn't realize what's happening. Vick keeps kissing her and she finally surrenders and starts kissing him back, never opening her eyes. Janessa is not even sure if this is happening. The kiss ends. Janessa forces her eyes open. The music seems distant and Vick's face is a blur. She is speechless and so is he. As she starts to get out of the truck, Vick grabs her arm. She turns around, expecting him to say something about the kiss. But he only tells her to get some sleep and he will stop by the office tomorrow.

"Anything else?" she asks.

"Like what?"

"Uh-um-nothing. I clearly need to rest. See you tomorrow" she stutters.

"Yeah definitely get some rest. See ya later." replies Vick.

Even though it's 9 a.m. she still feels like she needs at least another hour of sleep, but decides against lying back down. She admires herself in the mirror before leaving out. She sports a tan pantsuit with a tan and white abstract shirt and tan pumps. She drives to the office feeling refreshed and ready to work. She is taken a back to find Vick sitting at her desk when she walks in. He is looking through some paperwork she left on the desk the day before. She sits down across from him.

"Are you looking for anything in particular?" she asks.

"No, not really, just looking," he responds.

"Do things look okay?"

He finishes examining the papers, and gets up. He goes to the safe, opens it, and looks around. She watches, waiting for him to finish.

"Everything looks good to go," he says.

"Thanks," Janessa says proudly. "Hey, Vick?"

"Hey, Janessa." he winks.

"So last night, right before I got out of your truck ... umm," Janessa hesitates.

"Yes, last night when you got out of my truck..." he repeats.

"Nothing, I thought maybe I dropped my lip gloss. I couldn't find it this morning."

"Oh, well, if it is there I would have noticed it already, I keep my truck meticulous," he says.

"Oh. I must have misplaced it or something."

Vick brews himself a cup of coffee. It's already afternoon, and she feels like he's stalling. Vick doesn't drink it; and he hands the cup to Janessa. She takes it, and watches the cream swirl around the coffee.

"I know you have work to do, and so do I. I'm getting out of here," he says.

"Sure thing."

He leaves. As Janessa relaxes a little, the phone starts to ring. She answers, and finds one of her clients on the other end. It's the small Asian woman. She is amazed. She just serviced this woman a week ago, giving her enough supplies for a month. She tells the client to come on in, but informs her the price is going to be much higher this time. When she hangs up she smiles to herself. Neither Vick nor Malcolm has ever told her to raise prices under these circumstances, but she decides this should happen, and the client has agreed. She feels like she just made her own executive decision.

She's about to pick up her cell phone to call Vick and tell him, but then Malcolm calls. Janessa answers with an extra zing in her voice.

"What are you so happy about?" Malcolm asks.

"Oh nothing, just happy to be alive and well that's all," she quips.

"I'm sure not being a disgrace to your family, or in being jail, helps too."

"I guess so," says Janessa, sadly snapping back to reality.

"I was calling to check on how things went last night," says Malcolm.

"Everything went fine; the stuff is in the safe," replies Janessa.

"Good, good ... we need to get together soon."

"Sure. Is everything okay? Did I do something wrong?" asks Janessa.

"No, you're fine. We need to sit down and get to know each other a little better. Don't you want to get to know each other better?" professes Malcolm.

"Oh ... umm ... of course."

"Okay, I'll pick you up tonight then."

"Tonight?"

"Yes, do you have plans?"

"No, but I was hoping to get to bed early."

"You can sleep when you're dead. I'll pick you up from the office around 7," Malcolm rumbles.

She agrees, feeling she has no choice. As she hangs up her client walks in. She gives her a slight nod and goes to the safe. She reaches in and takes out a bag filled with small white pills. The woman hands her a crumpled white letter-sized envelope. Janessa opens the envelope and methodically counts the money inside.

"You forgot about what we agreed to?" asks Janessa.

"No, I could not take out an extra five hundred dollars from the bank without my husband noticing," cautions the woman.

"Well then, I can't come up with fifty pills for you on such short notice," replies Janessa.

She goes back to the safe and puts the bag of pills back in.

"No please, I need them," the woman pleads. "It's been a really rough couple of weeks, that's why I went through my supply so quickly. Please, can't we work something out?"

"Like what?" asks Janessa.

"I promise I can get you the rest of the money by end of the day tomorrow," she whimpers.

"Sorry, you're going to have to come up with something better. I can hardly expect a junkie to come through. Once I give you the pills, you have no reason to come back with the money."

The woman's lower lips trembles, and her fingers curl into tight fists.

"Junkie! How dare you call me that!" she shouts.

"That offends you? Fine, but what should I call you? You're the one in my office begging for drugs."

"I don't care who you are or who you work for, I will not be treated with such disrespect!" growls the woman.

She storms out of the office, slamming the door, forgetting the envelope full of cash. Unfazed by the woman's tantrum Janessa puts the pills back in the safe. She isn't worried about losing a customer. Where else will the woman get her pills? Certainly, not from some street corner dealer. Janessa smiles to herself as she recounts the money in the envelope. She is finishing when the angry woman comes back in.

"Yes?" snarks Janessa.

The woman slams hundred-dollar bills on her desk. Janessa calmly picks up the bills, and counts them: five hundred dollars. Silently she walks back to the safe, retrieves the pills and hands them to the woman. The woman grabs them and bolts out the door again slamming it behind her. Janessa takes out her book. She records what she sold, how much, and the price. She feels certain Malcolm and Vick will be impressed. She plans to make all customers pay extra whenever they ask for re-ups before they're scheduled. The rest of the day goes by smoothly. She makes several more sales, and by the time she closes shop she's made over six thousand dollars. She's just leaving when Vick pulls up in his Range Rover. Behind him is a white Mercedes—Malcolm's car. Both men get out of their vehicles.

"Hey," says Vick.

"What's going on?" she asks.

"We came by to see how business went today," he suggests. Malcolm is going through some things in the trunk of his car.

"Oh, okay. I thought you already did that today," she says.

"Yeah, but I got a call from one of our good clients complaining about some things that went down today," he confesses.

Sweat trickles down her spine.

"I can explain."

"I'd love to hear it. Let's go back inside" urges Vick.

"Okay," she says submissively.

Janessa clears her throat several times. As she and Vick go inside, Janessa sees Malcolm pull a black object from the trunk, and stick it in his waistband. This is the first time she's ever considered the possibility of these men doing her harm. They walk back to a small conference room and sit down. Malcolm starts looking through the record book Janessa uses, as Vick begins to talk.

"You look like you saw a ghost," utters Vick.

"I'm just a little nervous, that's all," she responds.

"Calm down, no need to be nervous, you're not in any kind of trouble," he insists.

Janessa relaxes a little, but then tenses when she realizes Malcolm has said nothing. Malcolm examines the book carefully. Janessa tries to read his face, but he remains stoic. Vick stops talking as he waits for Malcolm to say something. At last Malcolm speaks.

"Well, all I have to say is that she is going to have to get over it.

"You did a damn good job here, girl."

The corners of her mouth lift.

"You pulled in three times as much as we anticipated," Malcolm affirms.

"Wow, three times, huh? That deserves a reward," says Vick.

"I agree," replies Malcolm.

"What time is it?" Malcolm asks Vick.

"Quarter to six," Vick answers. "We got time."

"Plenty," says Vick.

She sits listening. They talk to each other as if she's not in the room.

"Aright then, let's go. Janessa, you can ride with me, and tell me how you did what you did today," says Malcolm.

"Where are we going?"

"It's a surprise, but you'll love it, I promise," instructs Malcolm. They leave the office together. Vick takes his black Range Rover, while Janessa gets into the front passenger seat of Malcolm's sparkling white Mercedes. Riding in such a nice car gives her a sense of privilege and empowerment. They drive off, Vick in the lead.

"She was livid with you for calling her a junkie," Malcolm observes.

"Frankly, I thought that was hilarious."

"Honestly, I don't know what came over me. I normally would never talk to a person like that." says Janessa. .

"Either way, you did your thing today. I mean, that's a brilliant idea, charging people double for re-upping so soon."

A moment later Malcolm's cell phone rings. He answers it through the radio in his car. Vick is on the other end.

"Hey man, which one are we going to?" asks Vick.

"We got hook-ups at both spots, so whichever one is closer."

"Aright, Route 40 then," notes Vick.

"Aright." Malcolm hangs up, and turns to Janessa. "So have you figured it out yet?"

"Not really."

"You're cute, but I think you know that."

"I'm okay," she replies with a smirk. She sees the bright sign of a BMW dealership, and sheepishly asks Malcolm if they are there for her.

"Who else?" he concedes. "We already got several whips … your turn."

"Any one I want?"

"Any one you want, with any extra bells and whistles you please."

Her tentative smile builds as the surprise sinks in. She knows she should feel guilty for violating everything she once stood for, and reaping huge rewards, but she doesn't. On the contrary, she's excited, elated even. As they park, Vick is already getting out of his truck. A Caucasian male in his mid-forties wearing a black suit and a loud orange tie rushes out to greet them. The men seem to know each other.

Malcolm introduces Janessa to the gentleman; whose name is Justin. They go into the dealership, where Janessa feels awed by all the expensive, beautiful automobiles. Glancing at random tags, she notes prices ranging from $55,000 to $100,000. As the men talk, she sees the car she wants: a black four-door 7 Series Sedan 750 Li. She motions for the men to come over.

"I knew you'd pick this one," states Malcolm.

"How did you know?"

"Because it matches your swag."

She walks around the car and peeks inside.

"You ready to take it for a run?" Justin asks.

"No need for that, we'll take it. There's no way she won't like it," opines Vick.

"Then why don't we step into the office and start the paper-work," Justin suggests.

"Paperwork?" exclaims Malcolm.

"What's good man? Your boss here tonight or something?" re-affirms Vick.

"Well, no, but after the last one I got into a little bit of trouble. Come on, man, I know you guys hook me up, but I do need this job," Justin tells them.

"Yeah man, we feel you," says Malcolm.

"Let's go in the office and do this paperwork," infers Vick. "Janessa, you can check out some of those bells and whistles while we're getting things settled."

Her eyes twinkle and she has an urge to run around the floor room like a child. The three men leave Janessa to play with the car. She can see them from the floor. How will she explain this expensive car to her family and friends? Maybe they won't ask, she thinks, but she knows better. She might tell them she's settled a large accident claim, or a medical malpractice suit, or a lead paint case. They won't know the difference.

She decides a lead paint claim is her best bet. The cut from such a settlement could easily cover a large down payment for this car. As she opens the driver's car door, the new-car smell overwhelms her. The black leather interior glistens. After sliding into the driver's seat, she turns on the radio. Bobbing her head to the music, she pretends to drive the car, even making car noises with her mouth. The blue glowing lights on the dash remind her of the buttons on the safe at the office. She is embarrassed when she looks up and notices Vick, Justin and Malcolm watching her.

"Sorry it took so long ... but it's all yours, bought and paid for," announces Malcolm, dangling the keyless entry.

Janessa beams.

"Thank you. This is unbelievable. Do I get to drive this outside now?" she asks Justin.

"No, I got a fresh one for you right outside, untouched and all yours," informs Justin.

"Wow, I feel so ... I don't know how to even describe the feeling."

Outside her shiny new car is waiting for her. It shimmers even in the darkness, and the chrome rims sparkle like diamonds. Janessa jumps in. She is as giggly as a kid on Christmas day. Vick, Malcolm and Justin shake hands. Vick gets in his truck and Malcolm in his Mercedes. As all three drives off the lot, it looks like a luxury car procession. Janessa contemplates whose house to drive to first to show off her new car. Vick calls her on her cell phone as she rides home.

"So how does it drive?"

"Amazing! It's so smooth I could go 100 miles per hour and not even realize it!"

"Well again, congrats, and you can be sure if you keep producing like you have, more rewards will come!"

Janessa happily cruises home in her brand-new BMW, hoping someone she knows will see her. She gets home in no time.

A few miles away Vick hangs up his cell phone and looks at Malcolm. "That didn't take long," says Vick.

"No it didn't. I'm not surprised, I knew that good girl act was a front," Malcolm responds.

"This is beautiful. She is going to make us so much money."

"Yep, and then I'm gone," indicates Malcolm.

"Man, sometimes I feel bad. She is such an innocent girl," Vick says.

"That bitch ain't innocent. Don't forget how we got her to work for us in the first place: she was stealing from me!"

"Hey man, I didn't forget, but we both know she's a good girl that made a mistake."

"What's up man? You got feelings for this chick or something?" asks Malcolm.

"Naw, not at all. I was just saying," says Vick.

"Look, don't be going all soft on me. You know better than anybody what happens to those that cross me. She was lucky enough to be in a position that I could capitalize on, otherwise all references to her would be past tense," Malcolm says sternly.

"I get it, I get it. Look, I'll catch you tomorrow," acknowledges Vick.

"Aright den. Peace."

In the parking space outside her home Janessa sits in her car a few extra minutes before getting out. The car has all the bells and whistles Malcolm promised: a navigation system, satellite radio, heated seats, heated mirrors, blue tooth, electronic starter and keyless entry. She can't wait to wake up and drive to work. On her way to work the next morning Malcolm calls her and tells her he is going to need to take her car for a few hours while she is working that day. She readily agrees, asking no questions.

A client is already in the waiting room of the office; a beefy African-American gentleman she doesn't recognize. She guesstimates that he is at least two-hundred-and-fifty pounds, and he is clothed in black, like a bar bouncer. His bushy black beard covers his entire face from the nose down. Despite his large stature his whiskey colored eyes are friendly.

"Do you work for Malcolm?" he pries.

When Janessa is hesitant to respond, he quizzes her again.

"Do you work for Malcolm?"

Again, Janessa doesn't respond.

"Wow, you are good!" he deems.

He gives a half smile and gives her a thumb up.

"My name is Big Mike and don't worry, Malcolm sent me here."

She peers at him and still doesn't say anything.

"Okay, I get it ... one second," he says.

He steps away and she can hear him on the phone. He steps back into the waiting room a few seconds later and hands her his cell phone. She takes the phone and immediately recognizes Malcolm's voice on the other end.

"Hey ... it's cool, that's my man. You can talk to him."

"Okay," she chimes.

She hangs up the phone and hands it back.

"What can I do for you, Big Mike?"

"You can start by letting me into the office and then offer some coffee, tea, water, something!"

"You're right, where are my manners? Please, come in and have a seat.

"What can I get you?" she asks.

"I'll take some water."

Janessa walks over to the area where she keeps the drinks and snacks. She grabs a bottle of water, pours it into a cup and hands it to Big Mike. She sits across from Big Mike, presses her one hand to her cheek and watches him chug down his water.

"I guess I should tell you the reason I'm here," he says. "In a few days you're going to be seeing a different crowd of people come through when you start selling that powder. Because of that, I'm going to be here to watch over things, make sure nobody loses their mind."

Fear overtakes her face.

"Don't worry, that's what I'm here for. Trust me, ain't nothing going to happen to you."

He lifts his shirt and exposes the butt of a handgun. She forces a smile.

"Look, when I say a different crowd, I only mean here and there," he goes on. "You may see some people who are little rougher around the edges, but for the most part you will continue to serve your doctors, lawyers, nurses, businessmen, etc."

"Really, they do the powder?" she ponders.

The corners of his eyes crinkle and he begins to laugh.

"They spend more money on this stuff than anybody else. I guess they feel their real lives are so boring they need to let loose occasionally."

"I suppose, but cocaine seems a bit much," she opines.

" I'm assuming you're no druggie. What do you do to relax?" inquires Big Mike.

"I like to jog."

"Well clearly that's not my thing," says Mike as he points to his sizable, rounded belly.

"It's not for everybody," chuckles Janessa.

"Show me the safe," Big Mike announces.

She opens the safe for him, and he goes through the duffel bag Vick left there a few days earlier.

"You know, we got to package at least half of this stuff before the end of the week," he says.

"We have to do it?"

"It's tedious and time consuming but it's gotta be done," says Mike.

"Do we have to start tonight?"

"Not tonight but definitely make room in your schedule tomorrow night. I'll bring all the packaging material."

"Okay," says Janessa.

Mike exits the safe. They walk back out to the front of the office. Mike tells her to close shop early tomorrow, around 3p.m., so they can get started with the packaging around 3:30. Mike hangs around most the day while Janessa services her clients. Eventually Mike leaves. A few minutes later Malcolm calls her cell phone.

"Everything good?"

"Yeah, everything is fine," Janessa replies.

"Are you done with the car?" she asks.

"Yes, it's in the garage, in the spot where you parked it earlier."

She locks up the office and heads to her car. When she gets to the parking spot she hardly recognizes the car. It now has dark tint on all the windows, the tires have new, even shinier black rims, and the car looks cleaner. Janessa circles the car before getting in. When she opens the driver's door a vanilla scent hovers in the car , one of her favorite scents. She also notices stitching in the headrest of the front seats. It reads "ESQ." The floor rugs have a cute zebra print with a hint of pink. Janessa is in love! A note sits on the front passenger seat. She opens it. "You're welcome, enjoy!" It's unsigned.

She sits in the driver's seat and takes it all in. She can't believe how beautiful the car looks, and it's all hers. She's even more excited at the prospect of showing it off to family and friends. She decides to stop by her sister, Angel's house. Angel lives with her husband, Darnell, a Baltimore City fire fighter, and their son and daughter. Janessa pulls into the driveway. Darnell pulls up behind her in his green Infiniti. His eyebrows squish together as he approaches the car. Janessa honks the horn, but he can't see in because of the dark tinted windows. She rolls down the window.

"Hey, brother, how's it going?"

"Whose car are you driving?"

"Why do I have to be driving someone else's car?" challenges Janessa.

"How else you going to be pushing an $80,000 car?"

"Maybe because I'm a good lawyer."

"When did you buy it?" he asks.

"Yesterday!"

"Wow! It's nice… it's very nice," he divulges.

Janessa laughs.

"Where's Angel?"

"She took the kids to get pizza."

"Why didn't you go?"

"I had to work late, but I'm about to get changed and meet them there, you want to go?"

"Oh no, I'm pretty tired. I just wanted to come by and show off my new car. I guess I'll have to send her pictures," Janessa suggest.

"She won't believe it. Congratulations. I fathom I don't even need to ask if business is going well," expresses Darnell.

"It's going wonderfully. Tell Angel I'll try to stop by again this weekend."

"Alright, I'll tell her, and again, congrats. I can't wait to drive it."

"Yeah, sure." Janessa waves good-bye and rolls up the window.

Her eyes flash with excitement to witness how impressed Darnell was with her car. She never considered herself a superficial person, but having the best and most expensive might be changing her mind. She drives home with music blaring on her satellite radio. She feels remarkable in her car. She parks, and gets out, all smiles. She gives it one more look before she goes into her apartment. She is opening her door when the phone rings. It's Angel. Janessa can guess what her sister is calling about.

"Hi, sis," she says with a smile that cannot be contained.

"What's this I hear about you driving a new black Beemer with black rims?" urges Angel.

"Yep, that would be me!" exclaims Janessa.

"Wow! You must be really doing your thing."

"Yeah, I just settled a large lead paint case, so I decided to treat myself," she lies.

"Man, I heard lead paint cases go for millions. Is that what we're talking here?" Angel coaxes.

"No I didn't settle anything that big. If that was the case, I would have taken you with me to buy yourself one too!" she replies with a chuckle.

"You better have," declares Angel.

"But it was enough for me to put down a large initial payment, and keep the monthly payments low."

"I'm proud of you, Sis."

"Thank you," Janessa gushes.

"I need to finish up at this pizza place and get the kids home.

"You're coming by tomorrow so I can see the car, right?"

"Absolutely. See you this weekend. Love you."

"Love you," mimics Angel.

Janessa stands at the top of her stairs with her palm pressed against her chest, finger splayed out. She gives a small yelp, which startles the dogs. "I can't believe it!" she says to herself. Momentarily forgetting the blackmail, the drugs, Malcolm and Vick, she begins to feel like a true success.

SIX

Big Mike is waiting for Janessa when she arrives to the office. She's surprised to find him there this early. .

"What are you doing here?" she asks.

"I need to do some security things. Some people are coming in later to install cameras, but unfortunately they won't be operational for another week.

"We're going to need all that?"

"Yeah, but I'm the most important part of the security," he replies.

He walks around, surveying the room.

"You got a piece?" he asks.

"A piece of what?"

Big Mike laughs so hard he starts to cry.

"Come on girl, I know you watch gangster movies."

"Not really," she says.

"Fine, let me break it down for ya. Did Malcolm or Vick give you a gun?"

"What? No. Why would I need a gun?" she fumbles.

"Man, these dudes really got you thinking this business is all rainbows and roses, huh?"

Standing in the middle of the office, she never thought this job would involve anything but selling drugs to the clients. Now here's a guy telling her she needs security cameras and guns.

"You okay?" asks Mike

"Oh, sorry," she says. "I don't understand... security, cameras, and now guns! I mean, I thought this was about making money."

Janessa's eyes turn glossy

"Hey, I didn't mean to scare you. You don't need no gun. That's what I'm here for. I was just asking, because, as your security, I need to know these things."

"Aren't you curious?" she ponders.

"Curious about what?"

"Why somebody like me is working with Malcolm and Vick."

"You mean working for Malcolm and Vick? No, I'm not curious. None of my business really. I just do my job."

"I see," acknowledges Janessa.

"I'm going to finish surveying the office so I can figure out where these cameras need to go," he declares

"Okay. Can I still work?"

"Of course. I'm not trying to stop the money."

"Great, so you do your thing and I'll do mine," responds Janessa.

Mike goes into the library and she sits down at her desk to go over the books from the previous day. She can hear Mike on his cell phone; he seems to be having an argument with someone. As his voice gets louder, he leaves the office, slamming the door behind him. Janessa continues to work. It doesn't take her long to finish with the accounting from the previous day. She'd done well, making the practice $8,500. Mike, returns, now calm.

"Sorry about that, nothing to worry about," he makes known.

"I wasn't," she boasts.

Mike goes back into the library and Janessa can hear the beeps of the fax machine. She starts making calls to some of her clients. She thinks it's a good idea to see if they need anything extra for the weekend. Just as she thinks about her bosses they both walk in as if she conjured them up. Vick looks extra handsome today. He has an amazing sense of personal style. Her eyes flicker with joy when she sees him. When Malcolm notices, they're flirting, he jumps between them. "Give her the box," Malcolm growls at Vick.

Vick hands her a medium-size mailing box. Janessa sets it on the desk, and opens it. Inside are several small vials with a slightly yellow liquid in them. The writing on the bottles looks like medical mumbo jumbo. She has no clue. Before she can ask, Vick speaks:

"After talking to several clients, I found out we aren't providing everything they want. There it is: now we sell steroids." Janessa examines one small vial.

"Our clients were asking about steroids?"

"I was surprised too. But apparently, that's the new thing now, especially among high school and college athletes," says Vick.

"But we're not going to sell it out of this office. I feel it will do better at our other office." Malcolm speaks.

"Other office?" she asks.

"It's nothing you need to be concerned about. We are only telling you about it because while we're getting things set up, you will see less of me around." Malcolm stresses.

"Oh." she responds.

Malcolm departs, going into the next room with Big Mike. They whisper about something, but Janessa doesn't pay them any mind. Affections glows in Vick's eyes as he approaches her desk. Her lips part and she licks them.

"So you're really getting into this huh?" judges Vick.

He leans up against the desk. She swings her chair around so her knee touches his leg. They're still chatting when Malcolm returns.

"Why don't ya'll just sleep together already, and get it over with?" snaps Malcolm.

Janessa and Vick both jerk away from each other. Vick quickly gets up and advances towards the door. She swings her chair back around.

"Oh no, don't stop now because me," announces Malcolm. Janessa can't tell if he's angry or joking. Malcolm abruptly storms out of the office. Vick turns to Janessa.

"I gotta run," advises Vick.

"Okay," mutters Janessa.

As soon as Vick exits, Mike suddenly emerges from the library, startling Janessa. She'd forgotten that he was there. He says nothing as he leaves. Janessa is glad to be alone. She thinks about Vick. Though it wouldn't be professional or smart to get involved with him, there's no harm in daydreaming. As she imagines making love to him, she smiles to herself, even getting a little worked up. Then a client walks in.

She serves the client, then falls back into thoughts of Vick, when her cell phone rings. Lo and behold, it's Vick. Janessa answers nervously, feeling odd about these fresh sexual fantasies. He makes small talk, and seems to have no pressing business. The small talk runs dry, and just as she hangs up, Mike barges back in.

"Is that Vick or Malcolm?" he demands.

"Vick," she snarls.

"Oh... okay," Mike says. "Everything cool?"

"Yep, everything is fine."

"Sorry," he says. "I don't mean to invade your space, but Vick told me to stay here if you are here."

"I'm fine, really. I know all the clients by now," she informs.

"Yeah, I know, but you're going to be seeing some new faces real soon."

"Are these new clients dangerous?" she asks.

"Yeah. Of course, you can't put anything past anyone in this business."

"I see," says Janessa her expression sobered.

"Hey wipe that concern off your pretty face," says Mike. "You'll be fine. Vick and Malcolm will make sure of that."

"Of course. I was thinking about what you said earlier,

sometimes I forget what we do here. I'm losing myself by the minute. I know one day soon I'm going to wake up in the fiery pits of hell," she vows.

"You can never forget what we really do here. That's what will get you caught. And as far as waking up in hell, well honestly I can't promise that might not happen to all of us." She can only sigh. Big Mike is right.

"What time you leaving?" he asks her.

"Soon. I just need to count the money and go over inventory."

"Okay cool, cause I'm ready to get out of here myself. I'm getting hungry."

Janessa counts the money as Mike watches over her. The final total for the day ends up only being $5,500, one of the lowest earning days she's had since she started working for Malcolm and Vick. She swiftly goes over inventory and closes the firm for the night. Mike and Janessa are about to walk out the door when Vick pulls up in a large, red pickup truck. Mike greets Vick at the driver's side window. He hands Big Mike a bundle of fresh one hundred dollar bills, and tells Mike to be at the office at 8a.m. sharp to help with a delivery. Mike takes the money, and bolts. Janessa and Vick are alone in the dark parking lot. Desire radiates between the two of them. Vick parks.

They walk back into the office, and he quietly follows her to the desk. He grabs her by the waist and starts to kiss her. Unlike the previous time, she knows this time is no dream. As they passionately embrace, Vick knocks a stapler and notepad off the desk and lays her down on it. He puts his hand up her shirt but she blocks him and stops kissing him. She lifts herself off the desk and sits straight up.

"What are we doing? Malcolm is going to kill us!" warns Janessa.

"Why are you worried about him? This is what you want, right?" asks Vick.

"I'm not sure," she takes in a sharp breath. "I mean, of course I've had my share of fantasies about you, but I never thought... you know... they could be real."

"Well, now it's real ... so are you going to live out your fantasy or not?"

He lets out a loud breath.

"Vick, I want this, but not here, not in the office," she sputters.

"Man, I should have figured you weren't for real."

"I'm for real! I just don't feel comfortable here, that is all."

"I'm sorry, it's just that it's been a long day for me and I was excited to see you and kiss you again."

"Again?" questions Janessa.

"Yeah again. I figured you were too out of it to remember the last time, which is why I didn't bring it up. But since then I haven't been able to stop thinking about it."

He grabs her hand and starts to lightly caress it. They start kissing again and this time Janessa doesn't stop him when he starts to peel her blouse from her body. They have uninhibited sex right on her desk. When it's done, she re-dresses herself at a distance and Janessa replays what just happened in her head. She fights back the urge to vomit.

"What's wrong?" he examines.

"Nothing. I'm fine." her voice cracks.

"If you're worried about Malcolm, don't be. We're grown-ups and we can do as we please. If it doesn't mess up business we good," he assures Janessa.

She finishes putting her shoes on. She closes her eyes and draws in a long breath. Despite Vick's reassurances she feels lightheaded and nauseous. He is right: they are adults and they should be allowed to do as they please, but for some reason she has a bad feeling about it. She knows it's not going to be that simple. He walks Janessa to her car and tries to kiss her goodnight, but she pulls away. On her drive home, she pulls over to throw up. The sex, the cameras, guns, and security: it all weighs heavy on her mind. Standing in the entry way to her home, she brings a shaky hand to her forehead and wipes away the sweat. She staggers to the living room and crumples to the floor.

Her phone rings; it's her mom. She hates to ignore her mom but she's exhausted and not in the mood to talk. She shoots her mother a text telling her that she is about to go to bed and that she will call her tomorrow. Her mother responds with "Okay" and tells her that she loves her. Janessa responds by telling her she loves her as well. She doesn't sleep well. In another crazy nightmare, she drives up to the house where her mother had lived before leaving for Alaska. She wants to show off her new car. She gets out as her mom looks over the car. Just then a masked man approaches, and pulls a gun. He grabs her mom, and demands drugs from Janessa. She tells him over and over that she never carries anything on her, and that he should let her mom go. The masked man doesn't seem to hear, and his demands continue. Janessa tries to plead her case, but then his gun goes off.

Janessa awakens. She doesn't know if the masked man shot her or her mother. Her blood runs cold and she is chilled to her soul. Her alarm goes off. She contemplates the nightmare and sex with Vick. She hates this roller coaster of enjoying her new life, then feeling guilty. She wishes she could silence her conscience, and prays this will get easier in time. On her drive to the office she calls her good friend, Gina. She's optimistic this will help her calm down. After several rings Gina answers. In a ten-minute conversation, they catch up.

When Janessa arrives at the office, it's business as usual. That evening she's finishing up with some last-minute clients when her office phone rings. It's Malcolm.

"Hello" she answers.

"Did you really think I wasn't going to find out?" Malcolm snaps.

Janessa's heart jumps into her throat and her whole-body shakes.

"Find out what?" she stutters.

"I'll be at the office later today; we'll talk then."

"O-Okay."

Her hands shake, and she's sweating through her powder blue blouse. She immediately calls Vick.

"Vick, Vick," she cries, "he knows, he knows … I knew it was a bad idea, what is he going to do to us?"

"Hey, hey, hey," Vick orders. "Calm down. 'He' who? And what does 'he' know?"

"Malcolm! Malcolm knows about us and what we did last night!"

"What are you talking about? No, he doesn't, unless you told him, and even if he did know, what are you so afraid of?" Janessa must think about that.

"See you don't even know" Vick points out.

"I know he runs things around here," Janessa remarks.

"Let me make this clear: he does not run things around here. I was the ears, eyes and mouth of this operation long before he was released from prison, and I am the reason he got released."

"Oh," says Janessa.

"Why do you think he knows anyway?" probes Vick.

"He just called the office very angry and upset." "It has nothing to do with me and you," assures Vick.

Her skin is burning and she begins to unbutton the top of her shirt. If it's not related to her and Vick she truly has no idea what's made Malcolm angry.

"I have to go. I'm sure it's not as bad as you think," reasons Vick.

"Can you come by the office?" Janessa requests in a shaky voice.

"I'm pretty busy, but I'll see what I can do. Relax babe. I promise you good."

She hangs up, and tries to concentrate on business. She goes into the safe and does another check of the inventory. She checks every item twice. She hears Mike talking on his cell phone in the library, where he always seems to be. As she nears the end of her inventory she must take a short break. Pain and nausea squeeze her stomach, and she sits down. Fifteen minutes later the pains have eased enough for her to finish up the inventory, but when she goes back to her desk, the pains return. Mike comes in; he sees she's in distress.

"You look really sick," he declares.

"My stomach always hurts when I'm stressed out," she confesses.

"Does this have anything to do with that fact that Malcolm is supposed to be here in a few minutes? He said he had something important to discuss. You have any idea what?"

"None," she replies.

It's almost time to close the office and Malcolm still isn't there. She bounces her knee and keeps an eye on the front door. She wants him to have forgotten about it, but then he walks in the door. He's dressed down in a pair of long, red and white basketball shorts, and a black t-shirt with the sleeves cut off. He stands there for a moment saying nothing. Janessa feels sure he can hear her heart pounding. Her stomach pains have come back worse than ever.

"You going to be sick or something?" Malcolm asks Janessa.

"No I'll be fine." she replies.

"Did you get some work done?" Malcolm ask.

"Absolutely. Everything is in order. We're on track to make $25,000 this week."

"Good, good."

Malcolm strolls over to the chair Janessa is slightly quivering in.

"Is it cold in here? Why are you shaking?"

"I'm afraid." she quivers.

"Afraid! Afraid of what? Me?" implores Malcolm.

"Um—well—yes."

He kneels so that he and Janessa are eye to eye. The jingling of his keys in his pocket is the only sound that can be heard in the room. He gives her a long, pained looked and then breaks eye contact. He genuinely looked hurt. Janessa had never witnessed this side of Malcolm before. The smell of cigar smoke makes her cough. "You have no reason to be afraid. I'm not going to hurt you. You're my ticket to paradise."

"B-b-ut when you called earlier you sounded so angry."

"I know. And I apologize for that. I was angry about something else and I took it out on you."

"You said you knew something." she states.

"Oh yeah that. Again, my apologizes. I was mistaken about what I thought I knew."

Janessa slightly moves her chair back away from Malcolm to increase her personal space. She wonders where the hell Big Mike disappeared to. She can tell Malcolm is lying but she certainly has no intention to challenge him on it. Quiet falls upon the office. Janessa is still struggling to get her bouncing stomach under control. She impatiently waits for Malcolm to say something.

"You say we're on track to make $25,000 this week huh?"

"Yes. One of our better weeks this month."

"You closing up for the day?"

"Yes sir. If you like?" advises Janessa.

"Yes sir?" chuckles Malcolm.

She feels like time is standing still and wishes Malcolm would do or say something that made some sense to her. He seems to be stalling, waiting for something to happen and the anticipation is literally killing Janessa.

"Hey!" booms Big Mike as he burst through the front door.

Janessa is so alarmed she lets out a squeal that causes both Big Mike and Malcolm to look at her strangely. Her chest rises and falls with rapid breaths.

"Everything okay in here?" Big Mike asks Malcolm.

"I thought so. But apparently, Janessa wouldn't agree."

"I'm sorry. I'm tired and a little overwhelmed." she says.

"I guess making thousands of dollars a day can get pretty exhausting." insinuates Malcolm.

"You know. You could use some help around here. Especially with what I got in store for us to truly maximize our profit." says Malcolm.

"You think we could make even more money?" asks Janessa.

"Without a doubt. Look if all goes as planned you'll be coming close to the finish line and be able to walk away from this."

"Seriously Malcolm?"

"Yep. Look, go home. Mike walk her to the car."

"Whatever you say, boss. You ready?" Big Mike says to Janessa.

"Very."

Malcolm has absconded from the office without a goodbye. Janessa tries to get her shaky hands under control so she can pack up her things to leave. She ultimately gives up trying to gather up paperwork, grabs her $1500 purse and departs the office with Big Mike. He walks her all the way to her car door. When Janessa arrives home, it hits her how lonely she is. Every night she enters her home alone only to be greeted by her two dogs Truth and Justice. She loves them dearly but to be greeted by a human presence would be wonderful. She hates the silence and sometimes it brings her to the brink of tears. All the money in the world can't erase the loneliness she feels on a nightly basis. She has become so consumed with the business that she has isolated herself from her closest family and friends. Her only real companionship was Vick but she knew that was superficial at best. She misses her family a lot. She used to spend so much time with them, but now she is always making excuses as to why she is too busy to see them or even call.

She has done a pretty good job at keeping how much money she has low key. The BMW has been the only major purchase she has made so far and she didn't even make the purchase. Of course, her family and friends have a million questions about how she could afford such a luxury car, many more questions than she anticipated. She never imagined that her story of settling a large lead paint case would become so drawn out and convoluted. By the time she finished telling the story she has come up with the names of doctors, other lawyers, and defendants.

Since she knew that none of them were going to try to look up the "case" online or in the court records she felt secure in her lies. The only person she has a few concerns about is her friend Gina because she being a lawyer as well, she could easily confirm or fail to confirm Janessa's story. Nonetheless, Gina and Janessa are very close and she has no reason to doubt anything that Janessa told her, and Janessa hopes and prays it remains that way. Janessa does plenty of shopping for clothes and shoes since she lives alone and prefers to shop alone, and nobody takes notice of how fast and upgraded her wardrobe has grown. She is getting quite anxious to buy something major like a large home or even send her mother on a trip to Greece. She figures nobody will make a major fuss if she bought something simple like a small townhome or condo, but Janessa didn't want that. She always envisioned a massive single family home with a beautiful yard and large extravagant rooms throughout the house.

However, if she purchased a $500,000 home nobody will believe she can make a purchase even after being in private practice for almost three years. Her family has no idea that she is practically debt free, including over $200,000 in student loan debt. Malcolm had paid off her debts so that she could focus on the business and not on paying back creditors. Thankfully, it was easy explaining to her dad and mom, who were co-signers on many of her student loans why the debt appeared as paid off on their credit report. Again, she lied to the ones she loved and explained that she had filed paperwork to have them released as co-signers and her loan company approved the application. As expected, they were beyond grateful and had no further questions or hesitations with her story, which was 100% practical.

Malcolm was "paying" her $2500 a week and giving her another $2000 a month to pay a paralegal and newly barred attorney to take care of the relatively small, but actual legal matters the firm handled, such as small claims civil suits and misdemeanor criminal cases. On top of the $10,000 a month they were "paying" her they often spoiled her with gifts and no doubt she was not reporting her massive earning to Uncle Sam. She deposited smaller "paychecks" of $3000-$5000 a month into escrow and Malcolm promised to write her a check for whatever she owed the IRS on that money at the end of the year. She certainly could never tell her family any of this, so she was having a hard time thinking of a plausible story to tell her family if she bought an expensive home. Malcolm said he will sit down and talk to Janessa about making big item purchases and keeping them hidden from family and friends, as well as valid excuses for how she able to purchase certain items.

Sitting on her $8,000 couch Janessa begins to reflect on how she could afford these things. They were all tainted. But oddly not tainted enough for her to hate them. She realizes she has long paid back what she had stolen from Malcolm, $12,433.25, to be exact. Nonetheless, there is no indication that the two men plan to let her stop working for them anytime soon. When she looks into Malcolm's eyes she knows full well that even $10,000 a week would never satisfy his insatiable appetite for money. Her only hope is that when they start selling the other stuff they will make significantly more money and finally satisfy Malcolm.

It's early, earlier than Janessa has ever been in the office. The birds are barely awake. Janessa enjoys the peace and quiet. Today is the day they start selling the "real" stuff. Big Mike has secured the place like a bank, with cameras, weapons and even a panic button under Janessa's desk. "How did I get to this place?" Janessa says to herself as she observes her surroundings. Every day that passes she knows that she is becoming more and more a shell of her old self. She remembers sitting in her old office excited to pursue justice on behalf of those who needed it. She wanted to be sure that whether the individual that walked into her office was the plaintiff or the defendant that she fought for them vigorously and effectively. Now, she is the one that may need a lawyer to do that for her one day. She lets out a loud sigh. Big Mike surges through the door, which is not unusual for him.

"Morning." he says.

"Hey," replies Janessa.

"So you ready?"

She doesn't respond. She only takes a deep breath and stares off into the distance.

"I'll take that as a yes." grumbles Big Mike.

"Yeah sure."

"Oh I almost forgot. I've been given strict orders to give this to you."

Big Mike hands her a large manila envelope. She carefully opens it and inside is a folded-up piece of paper. She proceeds to unfold the white paper. It's a typed list of instructions. It reads:

SEVEN

FIVE COMMANDMENTS OF BUSINESS:

5. Always maintain business as usual

No matter what is happening outside of the firm you must continue to maintain the business of the firm. You cannot discontinue business under any circumstances unless you are shutdown against your will.

4. Know your role

At no time are you to do anything without the approval of Malcolm or Vick. You may be the face of the business but you DO NOT run the business. We do.

3. Always conduct business as if you are being watched

No matter how careful we may be someone is always potentially watching. Be especially careful when it comes to technology, writing something on paper is easier to destroy than an email or text message. No formal "business" shall ever be discussed over text message or emails.

2. Only work with those who are approved by "Upper Management"

Vick and Malcolm are the only two people that can make any major decisions and we DO NOT under any circumstances allow anybody else to make decisions for us or on our behalf.

1. Money over everything.

She can't help but smile a little when she reads this rule. There isn't even an explanation after it as there is no need. It's become very clear from the beginning that money seems to be the only thing that motivates Malcolm. Vick is a different story. She can tell he covets money as well but not nearly to the extreme that Malcolm does. Janessa can sense Vick does this for another purpose although she hasn't quite figured out what that is yet.

"Everything good?" asks Big Mike.

"So far. But why are they giving this to me now? Why not in the beginning?"

"I don't even begin to try to figure out the inner workings of those two men's heads. I just do what I'm told and collect my hefty paycheck. You should do the same. Your first new clients should be here soon."

"Oh should I do something to prepare?" she asks nervously.

"Nope just sit there and look pretty."

The two sit there in silence, she drums her fingers on the desk. The client finally arrives. She grips the arms of her chair when a familiar face enters the office. It is her former real property professor! But fortunately for Janessa she did not have much passion for real property and sat in the very back of the classroom and he didn't recognize her or at least she didn't think so. Her eyes dart around the room looking for Big Mike. He has vanished and she doesn't know what the fuck she is supposed to do. Her palms sweat and her heart literally aches. The white haired, thick glasses wearing gentleman stands at her desk outwardly not the least bit nervous.

"Pretty nice weather we're having for approaching November and all." spoke the gentlemen.

"Um-um---yeah it's been nice. Not too cold ya know." agrees Janessa. "So...um...Can I help you with something today?" she solicits.

"I was hoping you could."

Janessa sits there like a deer caught in headlights. She methodically goes through the commandments in her head. Malcolm comes into the office with Big Mike following closely behind and saves her.

"Oh hey man what's up?" Malcolm says to the white-haired gentleman.

"Hey man am I glad to see you here."

"Big Mike get the man what he needs." commands Malcolm.

Big Mike exits the office and goes into the library and comes back out with three black pens in his hand. He hands Malcolm the pens. Malcolm in turn hands them to Janessa 's former real property professor.

"Same as before?" the gentleman asks Malcolm.

"Nothing has changed other than the location." responds Malcolm.

He hands Malcolm what looks like to be a credit card, then he gives Janessa and Big Mike a slight nod and leaves. Malcolm slips the card into his jeans pocket. Her forehead puckers.

"What the hell just happened here?" she shouts.

"You froze!" snarls Malcolm.

"Well...I...nobody...I mean..." stutters Janessa.

"Hey man chill. It's my fault. I never went over protocol with her. I'm sorry." expresses Big Mike.

"What the hell is wrong with you? You sampling the product or something!" booms Malcolm.

"Never that. Its home. Things have gotten bad again and it slipped my mind."

"I don't fucking care about what's going on in your home," counters Malcolm.

In response to Malcolm's statement, Big Mike's lowers his neck into a slow disbelieving head shake. It's apparent that Malcolm doesn't care about anything other than the business and making money. Janessa imagines he has many more enemies than he does friends and he probably prefers it that way. The expensive, imported carpet seems to sink beneath her $1200 shoes. Her eyes leave Malcolm and focus on her overly priced shoes. "When did I even buy these shoes?" she thinks to herself.

"Hey!" shouts Malcolm as he slams his large hand on the table. Fear twist in her gut.

"Yes?" whimpers Janessa.

"What are you thinking about?" Malcolm catechizes.

"I'm not."

"You're not what?"

"I'm not thinking." she stammers.

"Clearly everybody around here has gone fucking crazy." Malcolm stomps out of the office.

"That was all my fault. I dropped the ball. He'll calm down soon enough. Nothing for you to worry about." says Big Mike.

"You sure?"

"Yeah I'm sure."

"So…what's bad? At home, I mean?" she asks.

"You should know by now that nobody shares his or her personal life. It's all business around here."

"Oh." says a disappointed Janessa.

"Look, you go ahead. I'll take care of things around here."

"No. I should stay. Make sure no more clients need to be served."

"There won't be anymore. I'll make sure of that. Go okay." insists Big Mike.

Janessa can tell by his tone she will not win this battle and packs up her things and leaves the office. As she cruises home she calls and text Vick to tell him about what happened but he doesn't respond. Thinking about their relationship causes her eyes to roll. They've had sex three more times, but none of those encounters were as good as the first passionate encounter at the office. Realistically it's nowhere near a relationship. Janessa is not even remotely sure why she thought it could be something real. When she gets home she turns off her phone and sits in a dark room wondering when it was all going to end.

The next day, she doesn't make it into work until around 11 a.m. and Malcolm and Vick are there with Mike and some other men she isn't familiar with. They don't even notice her walk in and they appear to be having a very intense conversation. She walks by them and proceeds to her office and she overhears Vick mention something about keeping guard over the stash.

Now she knows why the conversation is so intense. When she closes the door to her office she immediately lays her head on her desk. She is exhausted because of her constant lack of sleep. She is just about to drift off to sleep when she hears the door open, which prompts her to jump up from her desk giving herself a bad head rush. She starts to rub her forehead to alleviate the pain as Malcolm stands in front of her with a "gotcha" look on his face.

"Yes you caught me sleeping on the job." says Janessa as she chuckles.

"Why are you so tired, didn't Mike make you leave early yesterday?"

Wow nothing gets passed this man, Janessa thinks.

"Yes. I've been having a hard time sleeping."

"Well go get a shot of espresso because we have a lot of work to do today and we will probably be at the office pretty late."

"I'll run to the coffee shop now."

"Good, hop to it and bring me back a blueberry muffin aright." "Okay."

Janessa walks out of the office and notices everyone is gone except Big Mike. She gives him a quick hello and rushes out the door to the coffee shop. As she is walking she recognizes an unusually high police presence. She has become accustomed to seeing cops around her office as it was very close to the courthouse, but today there were more than usual. When she walks into coffee shop her heart is pumping like she ran a marathon. She doesn't know why she feels anxious, but she knows she needs to get it together ASAP before she gives herself a panic attack. She rushes into the bathroom and splashes cold water on her face, which makes her feel a little better. She takes deep breaths and mutters the name Jesus, Jesus over and over until her heart rate begins to slow and she starts to feel a state of calmness come over her.

As she exits the bathroom there is a police officer waiting in line to order coffee and she stands in line behind him to give her order. He keeps looking back at Janessa as if he wants to say something to her. She is used to being hit on by police officers in the area. They hit on all the attorneys so she is never flattered by the attention. Even so, he is very cute and she gives him a half smile. He nervously smiles back. He orders and then turns to her and asks her what she will like. Janessa is surprised by the aggressive move after he acted so passive just a few minutes ago.

"Um a small dark roast coffee with two shots of espresso," she tells him.

"Two shots huh, must have been a rough night."

"Yep, party, party," she quips.

The coffee shop employee takes the order and the unnamed officer pays for his order as well as Janessa's. He reaches out his hand to hers.

"My name is Demetrius."

Janessa extends her hand to meet his "Janessa."

"Nice to meet you, Janessa."

"Thanks for the coffee. I guess we can consider this our first date huh." she smiles.

"Hmm okay that's fair. Even though it lasted less than ten minutes I enjoyed our first date," he muses.

"Me too."

"Can I call you possibly for a thirty-minute date?" Demetrius asks.

Janessa fidgets with her hair.

"Sure thirty minutes sounds good."

Janessa is unlocking her phone when it begins to ring. It's Malcolm.

Flush creeps across her cheeks and she answers the phone.

"Hey did the coffee shop get held up or something? What are you doing?" he snaps.

"Sorry it's busy in here. I'm on my way now," she informs.

"Okay, hurry up. I'm starving and need that muffin!"

"Here I come."

Janessa has forgotten all about Malcolm's muffin. She is relieved that he called and reminded her so she didn't walk into the office without it.

"I forgot to get my boss a blueberry muffin." she says to Demetrius.

"Out getting breakfast for the boss? That doesn't sound very fun."

"Oh no, it's not near as bad as it sounds. I offered, he didn't order me to do it or anything."

"Oh okay…can I get that number." He leans in closer.

"Oh yeah. That's why I pulled out the phone… don't take it personally but it's been my policy for a long time to take the number instead of giving mine." she attests.

Demetrius steps back.

"I promise you will hear from me." she stresses. "Okay I believe you, you ready?"

"Yep go ahead." says Janessa.

"443-..."

Janessa phone begins to ring again and again it's Malcolm.

"You're still there!"

"Yes, but I'm walking out the door now. I promise." Janessa hangs up the phone.

"I am so sorry he has never acted like this before. You were saying."

Demetrius stands frozen and stares at Janessa.

"Are you going to give me your number?"

"Oh my bad. I just figured if I opened my mouth your boss will call screaming for his muffin." he laughs.

"Ha-ha funny...well I really have to go, how about you just give me your card."

"No take my number, 443-847-6301."

Janessa hastily enters the number into her phone.

"Okay got it."

She rushes to the counter orders a blueberry muffin, pays with a 20-dollar bill without bothering to get her change and rushes out of the store. When she walks back into the office Malcolm is pacing back and forth and she can smell burned coffee. Malcolm looks up when Janessa walks in.

"Finally, you are trying to starve a brotha!"

He grabs the bag out of Janessa's hand.

"My bad it's really busy in there and I had to go back for your muffin."

"Uh huh I knew it! You are too busy flirting and forgot my muffin." he scoffs.

Janessa's back tightens; did he know she was flirting?

"No, I forgot that's all."

"Yeah sure, well let's get to work." as he demolishes the muffin she bought him.

"I'm ready," she says.

They walk back into her office, Janessa sits at her desk and sips her coffee as Malcolm begins to talk to her about how the cocaine they sell is kept in ink pens to give their clients the upmost privacy. The transaction between Malcolm and the real property professor all made sense now. Janessa is only half listening as she is still tired and waiting for the espresso to kick in. She also finds herself thinking about Demetrius. He is very cute and his shyness made him even cuter. She massages the back of her neck as she thinks about him.

"What are you all smiley about?" Malcolm interjects.

Janessa wakes up out of her daydream.

"Huh, I wasn't smiling."

"Look I know what I saw. Anyway, did you hear anything I said?"

"Yes the books must be kept separate." says Janessa.

"Yeah I did say that about 10 minutes ago…so you haven't heard anything I've said since then huh…. who did you meet at the coffee shop?" he questions.

"What are you talking about Malcolm? I'm tired that is all."

"Okay. You may not want to tell me, but trust me, I will find out." he jests.

"Malcolm I'm tired okay?" Janessa huffs.

"Can you give me twenty minutes please?"

"Fine. I got to makes some calls anyway, finish that coffee and I will be back."

"Thank you." she says.

"Yeah whatever."

Malcolm closes Janessa's office door. Janessa's shoulders slump. She doesn't want to talk drugs or money she wants to lay her head down on her soft pillow and go back to sleep. Within minutes she is asleep at her desk. She wakes up as Vick and Malcolm walk back into her office. As they talk about this and that, she doodles smiley faces and music notes on her desk calendar, and she starts to think about Demetrius again. She picks up her phone and sends him a text; it reads "how is your coffee officer? ☺"

She gets an instant response, which makes her smile. "It is great and yours?" She doesn't get a chance to respond back to the text because Malcolm starts to talk to her. Vick's facial muscles are tense. "Are you ready to work now?" Malcolm asks Janessa. "Yes of course. I'm always ready to work." she replies. "Good. Come on; let's go I need you to meet someone."

She gets up from her desk and trails behind Malcolm out the door. Vick also follows them out. They head outside to Malcolm's truck; she doesn't know where Vick went only that he followed them out. She and Malcolm climb into his white Mercedes. It has been a while since Janessa has been alone with Malcolm and she cringes as she enters the vehicle. The music's base vibrates throughout her whole body.

Malcolm doesn't say one word during the ride and Janessa worries that he may be mad at her. They arrive at Vick and Malcolm's office building. It's been so long since she has been there she has forgotten about the place. They pull in and she doesn't see any other cars in the area.

"Are they supposed to meet us here?" she inquires.

Malcolm doesn't respond, he is texting.

"Yeah, they should have been here already."

Janessa then notices a black car whipping into the gravel lot. They get out of the Mercedes and stand outside. Whoever is in the car doesn't get out right away and Janessa and Malcolm are left standing outside waiting. Malcolm starts to text on his phone again. She hopes that he is texting the person telling them to get out of the car! They wait a few more seconds and the person emerges from the car. It's a woman. The long-legged woman casually steps over a large crack in the ground as she approaches the pair. Her striking, bedroom eyes peer across the parking lot. One long, brown braid runs down her back.

The woman surveys her surroundings as she makes her

way over to Janessa and Malcolm. His eyebrows waggle as she approaches.

"It's so good to see you it's been way too many years!" she grins at Malcolm.

They begin to embrace and Janessa takes a couple steps back. The hug between them seems to last forever and Janessa continues to stand uncomfortably beside them. They finish embracing. Both of their eyes are wet. Malcolm snaps back and introduces Janessa to the woman. "Nicole this is Janessa, Janessa this is Nicole, also known as Nikki." The two women extend their hands in greeting.

Nicole cast her veiled glance.

"So you're the new me huh?" mutters Nicole.

Janessa's nose wrinkles and she doesn't respond. Malcolm starts to laugh and Nicole starts to laugh with him. Janessa doesn't join in on the laughter. They don't pay her any mind and proceed to walk into the building. The three go upstairs to the unsuspecting fancy office and Janessa begins to reminisce about her first experience in this office. She can't believe it's been eight months since she began working for Malcolm and Vick. The two women sit at the table. Nicole begins to unbraid her hair, exposing its golden highlights.

Malcolm hands both women bottled water.

"I brought you guys here today because now that Nikki is out I want her back on the team. She will be an invaluable asset." he vows.

"What is she going to be doing?" ponders Janessa.

"No, the question is what you are going to be doing that I'm back on the team!" pronounces Nikki.

"Hey , this is going to be an amicable working relationship, none of that Nikki." suggests Malcolm.

Nikki gives Malcolm the okay sign.

"I was joking. I swear. I'm not here to take your job honey, I'm only here to assist you. I know firsthand how exhausting it can be working for Vick and Malcolm."

"Thanks, some help will be nice." agrees Janessa.

"We're not that bad!" states Malcolm.

Both women give him a look as if to say "Yeah right." Malcolm flips them the bird.

"So Nikki, can you come by the office tomorrow morning so Janessa can get you set up with the pass codes and stuff?"

"Sure that works for me." says Nikki.

"Is there a time that works better for you Janessa?" Nikki turns to Janessa.

"Any time after 9a.m." she responds.

"Great let's wrap this up then. I'm starving. Can I take my two favorite women to dinner?"

Nikki smiles and at the same time says "No thanks. I already have a hot date."

"Fine how about you Janessa, dinner? We never did get to have that one-on-one meeting." he says.

Before Janessa answers she starts to think about what Vick might think about her going out to dinner with Malcolm. As if he is reading her mind he says,

"I promise Vick won't mind, it's just dinner."

"Oh so you're Vick's new girl huh." says Nikki with a smug smile.

Nikki gets up and leaves the room before Janessa can respond. She is blushing from embarrassment.

"No need to be embarrassed about it." concludes Malcolm.

Janessa's right eyebrow shoots up.

"I'm not embarrassed; besides I am not his girl." she maintains.

"Sure, you never answered my question, dinner?"

"I'm pretty tired and I think I'll just go home" she says.

"Okay suit yourself. For the record I am a much better date than Vick." he winks.

A smile tugs at her lips. They leave the office and head to the car. It's dark outside and Nikki is long gone. Malcolm is on his blue tooth making dinner plans with someone else, so he and Janessa don't speak on the way back to the law office. She texts Vick on the way back to the office. She hopes he can come over and keep her company. She doesn't hear back from him by the time Malcolm drops her off at her BMW. As she is about to drive off she gets a text and she anxiously checks it anticipating it's a response from Vick.

But when she checks her text it's not Vick, but Demetrius asking her how her day went and if she wants to have drinks. Despite being tired, Janessa does not want to be alone tonight so she agrees to drinks with Demetrius. She responds and tells Demetrius that her day was long but she will love to have drinks with him. He replies that he could pick her up and asks for the address. She gives him the address.

Janessa rushes home and begins to get ready for her date with Demetrius and she doesn't give Vick a second thought. She is sitting on the couch waiting for Demetrius when her phone rings.

"Demetrius!" she chimes as she picks up the phone without looking at her caller ID.

"Demetrius?" Vick asks.

"Oh sorry Vick. I was expecting a call from someone else."

"I see. Someone named Demetrius huh." Vick responds "Well... um...yes." she mutters.

"Hmmm. I won't ask any more questions. You can do as you wish if it doesn't interfere with business of course."

"Of course."

"By the way, sorry I didn't call earlier but I am seeing your text for the first time. You still want me to come over?" he asks.

"Actually I think I'm going to call it an early night. You saw how bad I was struggling to stay awake today. I could use the rest."

"Yeah, you're right. I should probably do the same thing; I'll see you tomorrow then."

As soon as Janessa hangs up the phone with Vick, Demetrius calls.

"Hi, are you outside" she asks.

"Yes ma'am."

"Okay, I'm coming down now."

She jumps off the couch and runs downstairs. Demetrius is outside at the bottom of her steps waiting. Lust glistens in her eyes as she takes in the sight of this ebony, toned, clean shaven man standing before her. They walk to his black pick-up truck. Although it's not the expensive and fancy cars to which she has become accustomed, it is obvious he takes good care of it. It's clean with tinted windows and nice rims like the cars and trucks Vick and Malcolm drive. Demetrius opens the door for her. Janessa is so short she has a hard time lifting herself into the truck. He tries to help her up, but ends up pushing her into the truck with his hands firmly planted on her ass. Janessa giggles.

"Sorry, I was trying to help. I promise."

"It's fine. I appreciate the assistance," Janessa smirks.

"Where are we headed?" she asks.

"This bar a friend of mine co-manages on Charles Street, unless you have some other ideas."

"No, not at all. Lead the way." she says.

The bar is only a few minutes from Janessa's house. They get there so fast that their conversation is limited. As they are walking in, Janessa thinks that she saw one of Vick's cars out of the corner of her eye, but she shrugs it off. The bar is bustling. She feels a sense of relaxation, which is something she hasn't had the pleasure to feel in a long time. But her sense of relaxation doesn't last. At the other end of the bar talking to a young lady sits Vick! Her breath shook and she draws closer to Demetrius. His brows drew together.

"Are you hiding from somebody?"

"No, why would you say that?" she asks.

"Nothing…hey, I see an old friend of mine," he says shifting his attention.

They start walking and to her horror they are heading straight toward Vick. This can't be happening; Janessa thinks to herself. The closer they get to Vick the faster and harder her heart pumps. She begins to drag her feet, but to her relief Vick walks away and Demetrius begins to talk to a bushy-haired woman standing by the bar.

"Hey, what are you doing here?" says Demetrius.

"Hey D, I should be asking you the same question!"

She gets up from her seat and swings her arms around Demetrius.

"Keesha, this is Janessa."

"Hi Janessa," Keesha says turning to acknowledge her.

"Hi" Janessa manages to choke out.

She can't muster up any more conversation as she cautiously scans the room for Vick. "I'm sorry, I need to go to the bathroom." Janessa rushes off. She prays that she can escape into the bathroom without running into Vick, but those prayers go unanswered.

"So you thought I didn't see ya, huh?"

Janessa jumps as the familiar voice whispers in her ear.

"Oh, hey Vick."

"No hard feelings. I totally understand…you don't need to explain anything to me" he winks.

Janessa can only nervously smile and before she can say anything else Vick disappears back into the crowd. She goes into the bathroom and freshens up. When she returns to the bar, Demetrius has a drink for her.

"Feeling better? I got you a Bahama Mama. Thought you might prefer something light."

"Yes, I'm fine…thanks. What did you get?"

"Henny on the rocks," he says.

"What do you think of the place?" he asks.

"It's really nice. I'm surprised I've never heard of it before," she responds surveying the bar.

"It's gone through several owners in the last three years, so that's why you probably haven't heard of it. Whenever the owner changes, the name changes too."

"I see… I like it. You said a friend of yours co-manages it, right?" she asks.

"Yeah, he must not be here tonight though because I haven't seen him and he hasn't responded to my text yet." Demetrius' voice fades away as Janessa begins to look for Vick in the crowd.

"You see someone you know?" Demetrius asks, noticing that she is distracted.

"Oh, no. I thought I did, but it turned out not to be him."

"Old boyfriend?"

Janessa chuckles "Not even."

They have a good time getting to know each other and drinking. Before she knows it, it's after 1 a.m. She knows that she must be awake and alert at work tomorrow, especially with Nikki hovering around. She tells Demetrius that she needs to go home and he pays the tab so they can head out. As they are leaving, she sees Vick again, this time standing outside the bar. He's talking to another young woman this time. Janessa is glad that Vick saw her out with another guy. He gives her a sly smile and a wink as they walk by. Demetrius walks slightly ahead of Janessa then he turns around realizing that he has walked a few steps in front of her, stopping to wait for her to catch up.

"Sorry, people always complain about how fast I walk. I really don't walk that fast, I just have a long stride." Demetrius explains.

"No problem. I get the opposite complaint that I walk too slow!" Janessa jokes.

Demetrius must help Janessa into the passenger seat again of the large truck. This time he avoids using her ass as leverage. They continue to talk on the ride back to Janessa's apartment. The conversation flows easily and Janessa feels very comfortable with Demetrius even though this is only their first date.

"You have to work in the morning, right?" Demetrius asks.

"Yes, unfortunately. How about you?"

"I work tomorrow, but I work the night shift so I don't have to go in until 4 p.m."

"Oh, nice…so you keep me up late and you get to sleep in!" she quips.

"I'm sorry. That is pretty inconsiderate of me."

"It's okay. I had a great time, so it's worth being tired tomorrow."

"Good, that makes me feel better."

Demetrius leans in for a kiss but he's interrupted by Janessa's blaring ring tone. Janessa sends the call to voicemail.

"I suppose that's dad telling you it's time to come in, huh." Demetrius laughs.

"Yeah right, but I do need to get some sleep though."

"Goodnight. I will give you a call tomorrow," he says.

"Okay. Thanks again and goodnight."

Her phone rings again as she walks into her apartment. It's Vick. This time she answers it.

"So, is he spending the night?"

"Ha ha, very funny… is she spending the night?" she asks back.

"I asked first."

"No he is not spending the night. I'm going to bed so I can be productive tomorrow at work," she answers.

"You claimed you were so tired when I offered to come over, but you seemed wide awake at the bar."

"Vick about that…"

"You know what, you are a grown and single woman. You can do whatever you like. All I'm saying is, I never want you to feel like you need to lie to me."

"I hear you. I'm going to get some rest. I'll see you tomorrow," she responds.

"Cool, see you tomorrow…goodnight."

Janessa wakes up the next morning feeling refreshed and ready to work. When she arrives at the office she is surprised to find that she is the first one there. She turns on the lights and boots up her computer. She decides against spending money on coffee and she makes her coffee in the office. As she is sipping her unimpressive coffee she gets a text from Demetrius wishing her a good morning and good day. Janessa smiles and texts him back "Ditto." She is anxious to impress Nikki today. Janessa is finishing her coffee when Nikki walks into her office. She is nicely dressed wearing a sharp dark blue suit and a flowery blouse underneath her jacket. Janessa blushes with embarrassment. She is only wearing a pair of black slacks and a green shirt that is a little too casual for work.

"Good morning," Nikki says, giving Janessa a once over and smirking a little.

"Good morning, you look nice," Janessa greets her.

"Thanks, I love dressing up whenever I can. I see they have changed the dress code this time," Nikki snarks.

"Oh, I usually dress up a little more," Janessa says with a bit of a defensive tone in her voice.

"Hmm, I see. Well, shall we get started or would you like to finish your coffee first?"

"I'm done. Would you like a cup?" Janessa asks.

"No thanks. I don't care for coffee. I prefer tea."

"We have tea too."

"No thanks, I want to get to work," Nikki boasts.

"That's fine with me. That is what we're paid for right?"

"Right."

She gets up from her desk and walks Nikki to the safe behind the wall. She can tell that the safe and the organization of its contents impress Nikki. They spend almost an hour in the safe while Janessa shows Nikki where all the different drugs go, how they are categorized and inventoried, and how they keep track of what goes in and out of the safe. Nikki plays with her cell phone while Janessa continues to dispense the information to her. She can't help but be a little captivated with Nikki's seemingly easy grasp of everything she is throwing at her. They leave the safe and head back into Janessa's office where Malcolm and Vick are waiting.

"Good morning gentlemen," Nikki declares.

"Morning," both men reply at the same time.

Janessa holds up a finger

"Vick. I need you." she indicates.

Vick walks over to the corner Janessa is standing at. He gently touches her arm.

"What do you need?"

"I wanted you to make sure everything looked good." Janessa motions toward the safe.

"Uh-huh," Nikki grunts.

"I can't look at it right now. I know we just got here, but something came up and we gotta go. We'll be back later." Vick says heading out with Malcolm.

Janessa and Nikki go back into the safe with the list of clients who are supposed to be coming that day. They start pulling out product in silence. After about five minutes Nikki finally asks," I have to know what made a goody two shoes such as yourself get involved in something like this?"

"Bad luck I suppose," Janessa answers.

"Wow, that's some kind of bad luck."

"Well, more like bad choices," Janessa clarifies.

"I honestly couldn't imagine what kind of bad choices or luck landed you here," Nikki muses.

"What about you? What's your story?" Janessa asks trying to make conversation.

"I was destined to end up working with people like Vick and Malcolm,"

"We couldn't be more different," Janessa replies.

"It's funny how life works, because even though our backgrounds are night and day we are now the same kind of people," Nikki observes as they continue to pull products.

"What kind of people would those be?" Janessa asks. "People who don't give a fuck. Who don't care about the next person, just ourselves. It's the only kind of person you can be to be successful in the business."

Janessa is silent as she takes in what Nikki just said. She never considered herself to be that type of person. She cared about the next person. As she continues to digest Nikki's comments, she realizes she is exactly the type of person Nikki said she was. She has completely isolated herself from her family the last eight months, she hadn't used any of her money to help others, and her only focus has been the business and the money. She didn't care about the negative impact her work had on the people she was selling drugs to or the community.

"Hello, earth to Janessa!" Nikki exclaims.

"Sorry, I'm here. I was thinking about what you said." she says, her thoughts coming back to the present.

"You never thought about it that way, did ya?" Nikki questions rhetorically.

"No, I hadn't, but I guess you're right."

"Yeah, I hate to tell you but there is no way to be successful in the business and not literally turn into a monster."

"A monster?" Janessa ponders.

Nikki stops speaking and continues to pull inventory for the day's clients. Normally Janessa would have probed more, but this time she didn't want to hear anymore. She wanted to get their work done and go home. She and Nikki work like dogs throughout the day, and by lunchtime she is already exhausted. Nikki is very meticulous about her job and works very hard. She seems to be determined to outshine Janessa. She is overwhelmed with trying to keep up and not let Nikki make her look bad. Vick comes back into the office to check on things. He directs all his questions and comments towards Nikki, Janessa gives Vick a frosty look.

Janessa swears she notices a little smirk on Nikki's face.

"Janessa." says Vick.

"What's up?" she responds.

"Let's go for a walk." he says to Janessa.

Nikki rolls her eyes when hearing his suggestion, but now Janessa is the one with a smirk on her face.

"Sure, want to go grab something from the coffee shop?" she asks.

"Cool." he then turns to Nikki, "hey, we'll only be a few minutes. Stay here and serve the clients."

"Whatever you say Vick," she mutters.

Janessa's hand is casually anchored to her hip and her chin high as she is escorted out of the office by Vick.

"How are things with Nikki? Are you okay working with her? How do you feel about us bringing her in?"

"She's good. She knows the biz which makes things a lot easier because I don't have to explain or teach anything. I think we'll get along just fine."

"Great," Vick says with relief in his voice.

They are standing outside the coffee shop and have yet to go inside.

"Did you actually want something?" Vick asks.

"No, not really."

"Well, let's go back to the office then. I didn't want anything either, I only wanted to talk to you alone."

When they get back to the office Janessa is not thrilled to see Nikki sitting at her desk on the phone. Nikki doesn't look up and she continues to talk on the phone. Janessa is not sure if she is doing this on purpose or if she is truly working so hard she doesn't notice them. She finally looks up and acknowledges that they are back.

"Oh, hey guys, I didn't hear you come in."

"It's cool. I don't mind if you're working hard" Vick responds.

"Yep, that's all I know how to do," she replies with a smile.

"You guys finished plotting my demise?" she chuckles.

Vick ignores her sarcastic question.

"I have to go meet with some people on the other side of town, you guys are good to finish up here right?" he asks.

"Yes," the two women respond in unison.

"Good," Vick confirms as he leaves the office.

"He asked about me didn't he?" Nikki questions.

"Not really, I would say he was more checking on me."

"My name never came up?" insists Nikki.

Janessa draws in a long breath.

"Yes, your name came up."

"And?" Nikki presses.

"And...he wanted to know how we were getting along. That's all," she responds.

"What did you say?"

"I said things were going fine and I was happy to have you on board."

Nikki purses her lips and sucks her teeth.

"What, you don't believe me?" Janessa debates.

"If you say that's what happened, then that's what happened," Nikki retorts back.

Nikki gets up from Janessa's desk and motions to the chair, letting her know that she could have it back. She obliges, walking over to her chair and taking a seat.

"Now that we're best friends, I guess I can let you in on a little secret."

Janessa sits up in anticipation of hearing this big secret, but Nikki doesn't say anything. The two sit in silence for a few seconds and as Nikki is about to say something there is a loud knock at the door. Both women recoil. Their clients do not knock with such authority. Nikki walks over to the door and opens it. It's Janessa's good friend Gina.

"Gina?" Janessa jerks back and there is a rise in her vocal pitch.

"Hey girl. I'm sorry to barge in on you like this. I have some big news!"

Gina realizes that she and Janessa are not the only ones in the room.

"This is my new paralegal Nikki."

"Hi Nikki."

"Hi, nice to meet you. I was leaving to file some things at the court. I'll be back." Nikki says.

"Okay." Janessa replies as Nikki leaves the office.

"So what's the big news?"

"I got the job with the U.S. Attorney's Office!"

"That's great! That took forever."

"Six months! But it was well worth it. Now we both have our dream jobs!"

"That's awesome. What division?" Janessa asks.

"Criminal. Exactly what I wanted. I'm going to be working to get all these drug dealers and gangsters off the streets." exclaims Gina.

Janessa takes a large gulp. Her face begins to heat up like a warming oven. Her breathing shallows.

"Everything okay?" Gina asks.

"Oh yeah. I'm so happy for you. I really am. You should let me take you out so we can celebrate properly."

"That's a must!"

Janessa can hear Nikki coming back into the office.

"I have to get some work done, but text me and let me know when you're free to get together for dinner."

"Of course. Talk to ya soon," Gina says walking out of the office as Nikki walks in.

"Is the girl talk over?" Nikki asks.

"Yeah."

"So? What's the big news?"

"My best friend is now an Assistant United States Attorney."

"Are you fucking kidding me!" Nikki shouts.

"What the hell is wrong with you?" Janessa shouts back.

"Malcolm and Vick are not going to be happy about this."

"What do you mean? Why would they care?"

"Why would they care? Why wouldn't they care?"

"I can't think about this right now. I'm going for a drive," Janessa mumbles as she hurries out the office. She stumbles to her car and speeds off. She drives much too fast through the streets of the city and has no destination in mind. She just drives. Today, she isn't driving her black BMW, instead she is driving her silver Porsche truck. No one even knew she owned it. She kept it parked at a private garage owned by Malcolm. It was another "good job" gift from Malcolm and Vick. She rarely drove it. "AHHHHH!" Janessa yells at the top of her lungs. "What have I done with my life!" she exclaims to herself in frustration as tears fall down her pink, blushed cheeks.

Anger, sadness, and despair rise from the pit of her stomach. She gags, but prevents herself from vomiting, as she doesn't want to make a mess of her luxury car. Despite the booming music coming through the stereo, she can hear her cell phone buzzing. She suspects Nikki has told both Malcolm and Vick about Gina and that she ran off. Her watery eyes are making it hard for her to see. She finally pulls into the parking lot of a small diner somewhere on the other side of the city.

The clouds float across the sky like delicate ballerinas. Janessa watches them dance across the grey and blue background. She searches her Gucci bag for a tissue to wipe her face. In between blowing her nose, she checks the missed calls on her cell phone. To her surprise there is not one missed call from Malcolm or Vick. The missed calls are all from Demetrius. Demetrius, the one bright spot in Janessa's life during the last week or so. He was so sweet, considerate, and honest. Nothing like the people she has surrounded herself with for almost a year now. Her mouth rises at one corner into a pleasant half smile. She tries to call him back, but his phone goes to voicemail. Sad that she was unable to reach him, her mood brightens when he shoots her a quick text telling her he's on another call and he will call her when he is done.

EIGHT

The next day Janessa is completely unmotivated. She can't understand why the time is passing so slow. It's 4:30 p.m. and she can't wait for 6 p.m. to roll around so she can leave. She used to leave at 5 p.m., but Malcolm and Vick decided it would be best for her to stick around an extra hour for clients who didn't get off until 5 p.m. Malcolm initially wanted her at the office until 7 p.m., but Vick talked him down to 6 p.m. They finally wrap-up for the day and she can't wait to go home. She and Nikki are waiting around for Malcolm or Vick to stop by and look at the books. Suddenly, a young, disheveled white woman walks into the office.

"We were just closing up. Can we be of some assistance to you?" Nikki asks the young lady.

"I need a fix now," the unknown woman replies.

"We don't provide fixes here. If you haven't noticed this is a law office, ma'am."

"Are you sure?" the woman presses.

"Yes, and I am going to have to ask you leave now," Nikki says calmly.

Nikki then motions for Mike to come over and chaperon the young lady out the office. Mike begins to walk over but before he can escort her out she turns around and leaves on her own.

"Everything good?" Mike asks.

"Yes, everything is fine now. Next time move a little faster, will ya?"

"Seriously?"

"Yes, you should have been pushing her out the door and sending a message that we don't take kindly to uninvited guests." Nikki scolds.

Nikki's face is red and she is tugging at the sleeves of her blouse. Mike doesn't dare argue with her. Mike assures her that next time he will be there to escort the person out.

"Good," says Nikki.

"What was that about? Janessa asks turning to Nikki.

"Mike knows better than that." Nikki proclaims.

"No, not Mike, the girl. Where did she come from? She is not one of our regulars."

"Oh, I figured this would happen. People get to talking, but we've been here before. Trust me we know how to keep it under wraps."

"Good, I really don't want people like "that" coming into the office,"

"People like that huh? Don't you realize we serve people like "that" everyday?" Nikki say sarcastically.

"She looks nothing like the kind of people we serve." replies Janessa.

"She is exactly the kind of people we serve the only difference is she is not wearing a nice suit, or $500 jeans, but at the end of the day they are all the same kind of people, DRUG ADDICTS!"

Vick finally shows up to go over the books for the day.

"Hey ladies, how's it going? How much money did we make today?" he asks.

"Actually, we were over our expected total by $5,000." Janessa concludes.

He quietly looks over the books and then looks inside the safe. "Let's get out of here. I'll take the books home to review." Vick says.

"Hey Mike, let's go," he yells over to the library where Mike is sitting.

Janessa strolls over to the refrigerator and takes out a small bottle of water. She begins to chug down the water making loud gulping noises as she drinks. Lately coffee has been her main source of hydration, making the water taste that much better. Janessa finishes the small bottle in a matter of seconds and grabs another bottle. She begins to gulp it down as everyone proceeds to exit the office. They all walk to their luxury cars. Janessa to her BMW; Nikki to her Mercedes; Mike to his Ranger Rover; and Vick to his Bentley. She drives home with the no radio, enjoying the peace and quiet. When she is almost home, Demetrius texts her asking how her day went. She is excited to hear from him. She responds that her day was productive and asks him about his.

He responds the same and then asks if she would like to go with him to get some dinner. The thought of leaving her home again after such a long day doesn't sound very appealing, but she doesn't want to say no. Nonetheless, she is very tired. She knows that she would not be good company and declines his offer. Even though they are communicating through text, she can tell he is disappointed. Janessa quickly walks the dogs and skips dinner in favor of her bed. She is climbing into her bed when her phone rings. It's Malcolm. She ignores it and lets it go to voicemail. He calls again and again. Janessa realizes she has no choice and finally answers the phone.

"Hello," she says making her best attempt to sound like she was already sleeping.

"You need to get down the office now!" he says harshly.

She is so startled that she chokes on her own saliva. She starts to cough furiously.

"Hello? Hello? You there?" Malcolm asks.

In between coughs Janessa tries to answer.

"Yes, I'm here," she says.

" Be at the office in fifteen minutes," he demands.

She has heard Malcolm speak with authority and urgency before, but nevertheless she is frightened. She is getting re-dressed when her phone rings again. This time it's Nikki.

"Yes?" Janessa answers sounding very annoyed.

"Did he call you?" Nikki asks.

"Who?"

"Malcolm!"

"Yes and I'm on my way to the office...did you get the same call?" Janessa inquires.

"Yes. I'm worried."

"Worried, why?"

"Cleary you don't know Malcolm as well as you thought you did."

The phone goes dead. Janessa had forgotten to put it on the charger all day. She finally finishes throwing on some sweats and leaves her house. She jumps in the car and heads toward the office. Now that she has a second to think about what just happened she starts to feel a strong sense of anxiety. If Nikki is worried, then she undoubtedly should be concerned. She arrives at the office feeling a deep sense of dread and even sadness. She takes a breath, says a prayer, and gets out of her car to head into the office. Nikki is only a few steps ahead of her.

"Hey, wait up!" Janessa calls out.

She picks up the pace as Nikki stops and turns around so that Janessa can catch up. They continue the rest of the walk to the office together.

"So what do you think this is about?" Janessa asks.

"It can only be about one thing." Nikki responds.

"Okay, what's that?"

"Money," she says calmly.

Janessa gazes off.. They arrive at the office and Nikki unlocks the door. She didn't know that Nikki had a key to the office. She turns on the lights as they walk in. As many times as she has been in this office, at this moment it feels uncomfortable and eerie. Chills run up and down her spine.

" I guess there is no chance that this could be some sort of joke, huh?" Janessa says trying to break the tension.

Nikki's eyes roll into the back of her head. The room is silent until Vick, Malcolm, and Mike enter the office together. Their expressions hardened. Janessa's chest tightens.

"I can't believe that it has come to this. I thought we were a family to be trusted no matter what," Malcolm speaks.

Unexpectedly, Malcolm pulls a gun out of his waistband and holds it by his side. Janessa cringes.

"I am only going to ask once. Who took it?" he interrogates.

Malcolm marches over to Janessa, his every muscle tensed. Her nose is almost touching his chest. Smells of mint and marijuana smoke overwhelm her nostrils. Fear paralyzes her.

"My dear Janessa, you wouldn't betray me, would you?"

The room starts to spin and spots appear all over Malcolm's face. Then the room goes black and Janessa is being helped off the floor by Vick. She stumbles as Vick walks her over to a chair to sit down. Nikki brings her some water. Malcolm stands in a corner, his pulse visibly slamming in his neck. Janessa tries to quickly gather herself .

"You okay?" Vick asks. "You passed out."

"Yes, I guess so. Sorry."

"I suspect there may be a particular reason she is so nervous," Malcolm says from across the room.

Everyone looks over to where Malcolm is standing.

"Yo man, what's going on with you? What did you call us here for?" Vick challenges.

"The money." Malcolm says sternly.

"Money?"

"Yes MY money," Malcolm growls.

"What the hell man. I know I didn't get out of my warm bed so you could talk in code all night!" Mike barks.

Malcolm starts to laugh. Janessa is glad she is sitting down because she is sure she would pass out again if she wasn't.

"Malcolm, baby, have you come off your meds again?!" Nikki asks.

Immediately after making that statement panic assails her.

"What did you say?" says Malcolm between clinched teeth.

"I—umm said—umm—" Nikki stumbles with her words.

"Look man, you know she didn't mean it. Can we please get to the point of why we're all here?" Vick asks, the frustration clear in his voice.

"You know what man, you're right, it's been a long day for all of us, and we should be home asleep right now. Let's get out of here," Malcolm says.

Malcolm moves toward the front door, but no one follows him.

"So what? Are ya'll trying to spend the night here or what?" Malcolm prods.

"Man, please, you don't have to tell me more than once," Mike says walking right past the perplexed group and leaves the office.

"Would anybody else like to go back home?" Malcolm dares, opening the door and waiting for everyone else to leave, too.

Nikki follows and walks out the door leaving Vick and Janessa in the office. Janessa remains seated and Vick helps her up.

"Come on babe, let's get out of here."

Janessa is a thrown off by Vick's showing of affection.

"Come on you love birds, let's go!" commands Malcolm.

Janessa and Vick start to shuffle out the door. As they are leaving, Malcolm grabs Vick's arm and asks him to hang back.

"I'll only be a second, wait in the lobby for me." Vick informs.

"Okay, no problem."

Vick and Malcolm step back into the office. He is back in a matter of minutes and he and Janessa pedal back to their cars soundless. She could tell that he had a lot on his mind and she was too tired and confused to ask.

"You think I can sleep in tomorrow and come to work a little later?"

"Sure baby, sure," he affirms.

He helps Janessa into her car and gently kisses her forehead.

"Do you need me to follow you home?"

"You know I only live a few minutes away, I'll be fine," Janessa reassures him.

"I know, but with you passing out I wouldn't feel right if I didn't follow you."

"Okay, if you insist. I just want to get home already."

She starts her car and waits for him. He pulls up next to her and motions for her to start driving. She follows his lead and starts the drive back to her place. Janessa can tell Vick is behind her because of his green tinted headlights...which he says symbolizes money of course. She walks to the door while Vick watches her from his car. She can't help but be a little disappointed that he didn't offer to come up and spend the night with her. He had been acting so loving and kind all night. She makes her way back to her bed and tries to go to sleep.

The night's events cause her so much anxiety that each time she closes her eyes she has yet another nightmare. She desperately wants to sleep and decides a glass of wine might do the trick. While she is in the kitchen getting a glass out of the cupboard, she becomes conscious that her kitchen is much too large and extravagant for someone who rarely cooks. She purchased a large single family home only about two weeks ago. And she didn't even have to lie to her family and friends about how she could afford it because she got the home at a foreclosure auction for more than a steal.

She observes her surroundings and realizes that there is truly no reason why a single person needs a 7,500-square foot home. The only reason she purchased it was because she could. Money and things had engulfed her life. She never wanted to be that kind of person, but here she was in her big house with expensive furniture, driving an expensive car, and having nothing else. No husband, no kids, and certainly no peace of mind.

Her family and friends are starting to inquire more and more about her behavior and spending habits. She doesn't know how much longer she can continue to lie to them about her life. She wants out, but she is sure that Vick and Malcolm will not let her walk away on her own terms. As the wine finally starts to calm her nerves, her thoughts travel to Demetrius. She could tell he was special. He made it a point to text her every morning to wish her a good day no matter what time his shift ended the night before. He always had a compliment for her and his smile was inviting and warm, making Janessa feel like they have known each other for years.

The next morning, she smiles as the foam forms on her mouth from her teeth whitening toothpaste. She just received her good morning, have a nice day text from Demetrius. Dating Demetrius has Janessa wondering why she ever dealt with a jerk like Vick. He didn't even call to check on her this morning. "What a jerk!" she says to herself in the mirror. She spits the white foam into the sink and flushes her mouth with warm water. She takes her time getting ready. She doesn't care how late she gets there. Still, come 11 o'clock Janessa is shocked to not have gotten a call or text from Malcolm, Vick, or even Nikki.

Fully dressed, she lays on the couch contemplating taking the money out of the safe in her home and leaving the country. The longer she lies there, the more appealing she finds the whole idea. She has the cash to disappear. But she couldn't or wouldn't put her family through that, leaving them to wonder where she was and if she was alive or dead. She also couldn't in good conscience leave Truth and Justice to be taken care of by anyone other than herself. It was a nice thought while it lasted, but it wasn't realistic. Janessa was sure even fleeing the country wouldn't prevent Malcolm or Vick from tracking her down. Janessa continues to lie on the couch with no motivation to go to work. She can hear her phone upstairs repeatedly ringing. "Leave me alone!" she screams at the top of her lungs. Truth and Justice come running out of their bedroom. "Sorry guys didn't mean to scare you." She gets up off the coach and as she is about to make her way upstairs her doorbell rings.

She opens the door to find two police officers standing before her. They are both Caucasian males and one looks like he should be in high school, not in a police uniform. The young one speaks first.

"Is everything okay here ma'am?" he asks.

"Everything is fine officer. Why?"

The older officer speaks now.

"We got a call of a woman sounding in distress at this residence."

Janessa blankly stares at both officers. Then she remembers screaming, "leave me alone."

"I'm sorry that you guys had to come out. That was my television the neighbors heard, not me."

"You sure?" asks the older officer.

"Yes, I'm sure. I'm actually a little embarrassed."

"It's fine ma'am. We're just doing our job," the younger cop chimes in.

"Thanks officers, I appreciate it."

"Thank your neighbors. Most wouldn't care enough to call at all," the older officer comments.

"You're right, I certainly will when I get the chance," she responds.

She watches the officer's converse while they stroll back to their patrol car. She imagines herself running to them and pleading for their help. Pleading with them to rescue her from Malcolm and

Vick. But she knows that's not an option now. She's in too deep. She makes it upstairs to her bedroom and checks her phone. There are numerous missed calls, voicemails and text messages. She then notices the time and that it's almost 1 o'clock in the afternoon. She had no idea it was that late in the day. She wonders if she should bother to go to work at all. She is about to check the messages and texts, but her phone rings . It's Malcolm. She answers.

"Do you realize what time it is?" he asks.

"Now I do, yes."

"Where you at?"

"Home."

"Look, don't bother coming in now. We're lucky we got Nikki and she is handling things just fine," he scoffs.

"Lucky, huh?"

"Yes damn lucky!"

"Fine, I am glad you guys are so lucky. Have a great day Malcolm." Janessa hangs up her phone.

She sits down on her bed and closes her eyes for a few seconds. Her phone rings again. She fully expects it to be an angry Malcolm calling her back, but it's her sister Angel. Janessa is relieved to be hearing from her sister. It's been about a week since they last spoke and prior to Malcolm and Vick she would have never went so long without speaking with her sister.

"Hey sis, where you been? Are you okay?" asks Angel.

"I'm fine. I'm sorry I haven't been in touch. I've been really busy with work."

"That's been your excuse for damn near a year now" Angel says with a heavy sigh.

"I know, but it's true. You should know better than anyone how much work it takes to get a new business off the ground" Janessa tries to cover herself.

Angel is silent for a second.

"Well that's true. Mom and I were talking about you the other night. She is concerned about you too."

"I appreciate all the concern. Let's do something this weekend including the kids. I do miss you guys."

"Oh sis, you would pick a weekend that no one is available. Your nephew is going to be out of town with his grandfather, I have a wedding to do on Saturday and I'm teaching a small hair cutting class on Sunday."

The booming barks from Truth and Justice begin to ring throughout the large home.

"You stayed home today?" asks Angel.

"Yes, I took a mental health day," Janessa laughs.

"Good. I gotta go, but we'll talk soon right?"

"Absolutely."

Janessa walks back to her front door. Truth and Justice chase behind her. Andy, Truth and Justice's dog walker, is at the door. Janessa opens the door to let Andy in.

"Hey Andy, why are you ringing the doorbell?" she asks.

"I saw your car in the driveway, I didn't want to walk in if you were home."

"Oh I see. Well just pretend like I'm not here and do what you usually do."

"Okay, no problem," Andy says going on about her usual routine.

The dogs are obviously excited to see her. After briefly greeting them, she goes into the back room to get their leashes. Janessa is about to close the front door when someone pushes it open again.

She jumps back. It's Vick.

"So you playing hooky, huh?" he says as he lets himself into Janessa's home.

"Come on in please," she says sarcastically, closing the door behind him.

"Why, thank you. Don't mind if I do," Vick responds back matching her tone.

"What's going on with you?" he asks as they walk toward the dining area.

"You know; you are the second person to ask me that today."

"So what's the verdict?"

"What's wrong with me is that I need a break, that's all. You saw what happened last night." She shuddered thinking back over the events just hours before.

"Yeah, that was pretty scary. To be honest, I knew from the beginning that you would only be able to handle this lifestyle for so long. That's why we brought Nikki back...to eventually take over things." he says.

"Things are getting too stressful and weird for me."

"Weird?" Vick responds.

"That stunt Malcolm pulled last night, Nikki's comment about medication, and then there was a strange woman who came into the office," Janessa explains.

"What strange woman?" Vick quizzes.

"Nothing," she brushes him off wishing she hadn't mentioned it.

"I think you've done enough. I think you've paid your debt back three-fold. But unfortunately, the final decision is not up to me. It wasn't my money you stole."

Janessa feels the liquid begin to well in her eyes. She closes them and rolls them back and forth trying to prevent the tears from falling.

"He won't ever let me go, will he?" she asks Vick.

He takes a deep breath.

"I wish I could tell you something positive, but we've made so much money. I don't think he will. Not voluntarily at least," he sighs.

"And involuntarily? How could or would that happen?" Janessa prods, looking for any way out.

"Jail or death. And I can promise you. He'll die before he goes back to jail."

Without another word, Janessa walks to the kitchen and begins to pace back and forth along the gold and cream tiles. The clicking of her flip-flops is the only noise echoing through her home until Andy comes back with the dogs.

"I gotta go," Vick says, heading toward the door as quickly as he appeared.

"Sure. See you later."

The dogs come bursting into the home energized from their walk and nearly knocking Vick over as he makes his way out.

Vick gets back to the office and finds Malcolm standing in the middle of the room nostrils flaring.

"What's up man?" he asks Malcolm.

"Man, you know what's up, so you sure she good?" Malcolm retorts through clinched teeth with clear restraint. .

"Yeah man, she good .," Vick reassures.

"Look, I have sources that say otherwise," Malcolm presses.

"What sources?"

"Don't worry about it. Let's just get to work"

"Where's Nikki?" he asks, realizing she's not in the office.

"I sent her on an errand."

"Well, what do you need me to do?" Vick asks trying to shift the conversation.

"I need you to do your job mutha fucker!" Malcolm rumbles at Vick

Malcolm swiftly walks over to where Vick is standing, his hands balled up in fists.

"Yo man, what the fuck is your problem?"

Vick and Malcolm stand eye to eye, fists clinched. Perspiration shows on Malcolm's brow. Nikki walks through the door immediately sensing the tension between the two guys.

"Hey, hey guys what's going on here break it up, break it up!" Nikki inserts herself in between them. Malcolm doesn't budge, his face contorted. Nikki turns to him, stands on her toes and whispers something in his ear. His face relaxes.

"I'm going to step out before I do something I regret." says Malcolm as he exits the room.

"What is going on with him?" Vick yells, venting to Nikki as she settles back in.

"I know what's wrong with him, but I can't say."

"What do you mean you can't say? I have a right to know," Vick presses. Her cryptic answers always frustrate him.

"Look I can't say. And you know better than anybody that there are no rights in this business," Nikki says almost scolding him for even asking.

"Fine. But can you at least let me know if this is temporary or should I expect this craziness from now on?"

Vick sees the concern spread across Nikki's face.

"I wish I knew the answer to that, but, honestly I don't know."

Vick throws back his head in frustration.

"I don't know how much more of this I can take,"

"Me either." Nikki agrees.

"Really?"

"Really. It's nothing like it was before. I almost wished I had stayed where I was," she continues.

"So, what do we do about it?" Vick asks.

"We deal with it and become millionaires."

"Why?"

"Why become millionaires?" Nikki smirks. "I'm going to pretend that you didn't asks that stupid question."

"No, why can't we become millionaires without the madness." Vick quips.

"Because he runs things. He's the boss, and that's how it's always been. Well, except for the years he spent in prison," she says.

"Exactly. Which means this enterprise can be run without him," Vick affirms.

"What are you getting at? This is your boy, your brother, we're talking about here."

"I know, I know. And I don't love and appreciate him any less than I did twenty years ago when we first met, but something is not right with him and it's making things more complicated than they need to be."

"So what are you suggesting?" Nikki prods.

Vick leans in and begins to write on a yellow piece of notepad paper. Nikki reads, her jaw drops; and with every sentence she reads her eyes get wider and wider

"You're serious?" she asks.

"It's unfortunate that it has come down to this, but yes I am, I'm very serious."

NINE

Janessa strips down to a pair of shorts and a Hampton University Alumni t-shirt. It feels great to be away from the office. She frantically cleans up, anticipating Demetrius' arrival. As she is scrubbing the last dirty dish in the sink, Truth and Justice shoot by her toward the front door. She knows it's Demetrius because he's the only person Truth and Justice don't bark at when he rings the bell. She gleefully skips to greet him and throws herself into his arms as soon as she opens the door.

"Happy to see me babe?" Demetrius asks with a glint in his eye.

Janessa plants wet kisses all over his face.

"Yes, yes, yes!"

They stumble inside her luxurious home and almost fall over the anxious dogs waiting for their greeting. Demetrius trips over Justice as Truth fights to petted first by their new guest. Janessa is still hanging on his neck when they fall to the floor together. Janessa's hearty laugh echoes throughout the foyer. Her laughter is cut short by Demetrius' lips beginning to caress her neck in her favorite spot. Tingles run up her spine.

"Let's go upstairs," she whispers in his ear.

"Janessa, what if I told you I love you?" Demetrius asks.

"I would say I love you too," Janessa beams.

Although she was only gone a day the office looks completely foreign to her. She notices that Nikki has moved her family pictures off her desk. She sits in her large, red chair in the darkness. Demetrius' words, "I love you," warms her soul. Only a year ago, she hated everything this office represented. The expensive furniture, the expensive rent, all paid for with drug money and she was a party to it. She has clearly lost sight of everything she stood for. She used to have morals, values, and a conscience. Not anymore. She boots up her laptop and begins pounding away at the black and white keys. This is it. She is done, whether Malcolm and Vick like it or not.

Her typing speeds up with every sentence . Emotions pour onto the Word document. One page later, the last words on the document are "I'M DONE!" Nikki comes in as she hits the save button. She slams down the laptop. Nikki looks like a true professional as usual. Light grey flared pants with a green and grey printed blouse. Janessa wishes she had a pair of those green and black shoes.

"Hey, how were things yesterday?" she asks Nikki.

"Things went well. We made almost $4,000 more than expected."

"Hmmm, oh really?"

"What you do you mean oh really?" Nikki counters.

"Nothing. That's really good for your first day on your own."

"Janessa, I've been running the business long before you ever came along. Trust me, making money has never been an issue for me!"

"You're right, I'm sorry I even said anything."

"What did they tell you about me?" Nikki asks.

"Whose they?"

"Don't play dumb with me," Nikki persists.

Janessa grins.

"They really haven't said much. Let me correct myself. Malcolm says you're loyal."

"Yeah, loyal to a fault. You know those two, nothing ever satisfies them, it's always more," Nikki says with a bit of sadness in her voice.

"Why do you stay?" Janessa questions earnestly.

Nikki is silent as she strongly considers the question.

"Same reason you stay. I have to," she points out.

"Fair enough."

At that moment, Malcolm bounces into the office. His fluid movements spell that he is in a better mood today.

"Good morning ladies!" he says.

"Morning ." Nikki responds.

"How are you this morning Malcolm?" asks Nikki.

"I couldn't be better. We made a pretty nice team yesterday, didn't we babe?" Malcolm says to Nikki.

"We sure did," Nikki replies.

Malcolm walks over to the cappuccino maker.

"Damn," he says.

"What's wrong?" Nikki asks him.

"We're out of my favorite cappuccino. I'll run across the street to the coffee shop."

"I'll come with you. I want a donut," Janessa chimes.

"Cool, let's go." Malcolm turns to Nikki. "Do you want something?"

"I can go too," she offers.

"No, someone needs to be here for the clients. Janessa and I can take care of it."

"Okay a banana nut muffin is fine," she says trying to mask the disappointment in her voice.

As Malcolm and Janessa are walking across the street, she catches Demetrius sitting in an unmarked police car out of the corner of her eye. He does a double take and then pins his eyes onto her but he doesn't say anything nor does Janessa speak to him. Malcolm and Janessa walk into the coffee shop and take their place in line.

"I wasn't surprised to hear that you and Nikki did so well together, you guys certainly make a good team," Janessa says trying to make conversation.

"We've always worked well together and she is the only person in this world I can completely trust. No offense to you, but she has stuck with me through some really tough times," he says.

"No offense taken. I understand. I mean, to make $6,500 more than expected is great," Janessa says, exaggerating the amount to see how Malcolm will respond.

"$6,500?" Malcolm asks rubbing his jaw.

Janessa gives her order. She tells the woman at the counter that she would like a caramel latte and a glazed donut, then Malcolm orders food and drink for himself and Nikki.

"I'm sorry Malcolm, you were saying something right before I ordered?" she asks returning her attention to him.

"Oh no. I was agreeing with you that yes, $6,500 over our goal was a great day. You know, these junkies are so unpredictable.

One minute it's a mad rush, the next its dead." he says.

"Just like a real law practice," Janessa giggles.

Malcolm fakes a smile. She can tell he is bothered by something. "Everything okay?"

"Things couldn't be better. Let's get back to the office. We don't want Nikki to think we ran off together," he says.

"Of course not." Janessa says with a slight smirk.

When they walk back across the street, she looks for Demetrius, but his car is gone. Back at the office, Nikki is already servicing clients . Janessa goes into her office to eat her breakfast and drink her latte. She is finishing up when she hears Nikki and Malcolm bickering. She laughs to herself and thinks hmmm I wonder what that could possibly be about?

Malcolm and Nikki storm into the office where Janessa sits.

Nikki is trembling with fury.

"Where do you get off telling such a lie?" Nikki roars.

"Lie?" Janessa feigns innocence.

"Bitch, don't you dare play with me. You have no idea what I am capable of," Nikki cautions.

"Malcolm, what's going on?" Janessa asks.

"You said that Nikki told you that we made $6,500 over quota yesterday."

"That's right."

"You know damn well that's not true! I said $4,000," Nikki screams.

Janessa gives a half shrug.

"Look, I'm sorry Nikki, but you said $6,500," she coolly responds.

Malcolm scratches his nose.

"Malcolm, I know you are not going to believe this bitch over me!" Nikki pleads desperately.

"I'm not saying who I believe until I look over the inventory and books myself," he responds.

Nikki's eyes swim with tears.

"Babe, by doing that you're saying that you might believe her. How could you do that? It's me we're talking about. I would never, ever, double cross you," Nikki pleads.

Malcolm can't bear to look into Nikki's crying eyes and shifts his gaze down to the floor.

"I'm looking, that's all," Malcolm says as he proceeds out of the room.

Nikki spins to face Janessa. She rolls up her sleeves and swiftly makes her way across the room to where Janessa remains seated and appears seemingly unbothered by the events that just unfolded in front of her.

"I always knew you didn't want me here, but to go these lengths?" Nikki says in disbelief.

"What lengths Nikki? Maybe you should be more careful about what you say." Janessa replies nonchalantly.

Nikki begins to laugh. "You won't win Bitch."

"Win? Win what, Nikki?" she asks.

"Okay Janessa, you have started something you are going to

deeply regret. I promise you that," Nikki threatens.

"Sure, Nikki. Sure," she gives Nikki a dismissive wave of her hand.

Nikki throws her head back and storms out of the office. Janessa pulls her cell phone out of her back pocket and sends a text message, it consists of just one word. DONE. She is expecting a return text, but instead her phone rings and it's Demetrius.

"Hey, babe. How's it going?" he asks.

"I'm not too bad. Just finishing up breakfast."

"Yeah, speaking of breakfast. I'm pretty sure I saw you walking to the coffee shop this morning," Demetrius says.

"Oh, so that was you! I wasn't sure, that's why I didn't stop to say hi." she lies.

"Right. The gentleman I saw you with…do you represent him?"

"Yes."

"Are you serious… you represent Malcolm Jacobs?" Demetrius asks.

"You know him?"

"Know him! I've arrested him at least four times. What are you doing representing someone like that?"

"What do you mean someone like 'that'?" Janessa asks.

"I mean, what are you doing representing one of the biggest drug dealers in the city?"

"Last time I checked I was a lawyer and that was my job," Janessa feels herself getting defensive.

"Why would he hire someone like you?" inquires Demetrius.

"Someone like me?"

"I'm sorry if I offended you. I am used to him using attorneys from those large, expensive firms," he tries to explain.

"Well, he did end up in jail for ten years using those lawyers," Janessa sneers.

"Apparently, they did work out for him since he got out on appeal," Demetrius snaps back.

"Look, who I do and don't represent is really none of your business."

"It is my business when we're dating," he says.

Malcolm makes his way back into the office and Janessa abruptly ends the call with Demetrius.

"Hey, come on out here I need to speak with you," Malcolm says gesturing for her to come over to him.

"Okay." Janessa gets up and goes into the office where they service clients.

"What's up?" asks Janessa.

"I looked over everything and it all points to us making $4,000 over quota not $6,500."

Janessa is silent.

"What do you have to say about that?" he stresses.

She throws her hands in the air.

"All I know is what Nikki told me. You are going to have to ask her these questions, not me," she says standing by her statement.

"I guess you're right. But I'll tell you right now, if I find out you lied about this whole thing…," he stops. Janessa doesn't flinch.

"What?" she asks.

"Huh?"

"What would happen if I did?" she asks.

"Nothing. Just do what I pay you to do and go take care of the clients."

"No problem," Janessa responds putting an end to the exchange.

She goes into the safe to get additional inventory. Nikki is in the safe too.

"Malcolm is no dummy. You will never get away with this," Nikki scorns.

"Nikki, there is nothing for me to get away with. You said $6,500. It seems to me that you're the one trying to get away with something."

Without warning Nikki rushes Janessa and knocks her to the ground. Her head bounces off the floor like a basketball and she blacks out for a second. When she comes to Nikki is on top of her, wrapping her hands around her throat. Adrenaline kicks in and Janessa quickly goes into fight mode. She viciously swings her arms desperately trying to connect with any part of Nikki's body. One of her fists at last connects with Nikki's nose. Janessa struggles to breathe when she hears a familiar voice.

"What the fuck are you doing?"

Nikki is thrown off Janessa. Mike has Nikki pinned to the ground as she aggressively fights to get him off her.

"Calm the fuck down! I don't want to have to hurt you" he yells.

Vick and Malcolm come running into the room .

"What the hell is going on here?" Malcolm bellows.

Janessa gradually pulls herself off the floor. Vick walks over and helps her up.

"That bitch is crazy! She tried to kill me!" Janessa struggles to speak.

"That stupid bitch is a liar and trying to bring me down—and the business too!" Nikki screams.

"Take her out of here," Malcolm says to Vick, motioning to Janessa.

Vick puts Janessa's arm over his shoulders and holds her by the waist as they retreat toward her office. Inside her office away from the others, Vick checks on Janessa.

"You okay?" he says in a whisper.

"Yes." she answers trying to pull herself back together.

"I told you this would happen and to prepare yourself," Vick says.

"What the hell took Mike so long?" Janessa demands.

"Hey, on the bright side things are going per the plan."

"Great, I'm glad my near-death experience has helped our goal," Janessa retorts sarcastically.

"Nobody said it would be easy."

"What would be easy?" Malcolm asks appearing in Janessa's office.

Janessa and Vick both gasp.

"Answer my question. What would be easy?" he asks again.

"Working in this business," Vick responds trying to think quick.

"That goes without saying. Are you going to be okay?" Malcolm asks.

"Yes, I'll be fine," Janessa assures him.

"I love that girl, but Nikki definitely has a very hot and short temper," Malcolm notes.

"What did you say to set her off like that anyway?" Vick asks.

"Nothing. I swear."

"I knew she might get jealous, but I never thought she would result to violence." Malcolm says.

"Where is Nikki now?" Vick asks.

"Man, she was tripping. I couldn't get her to calm down, so I did what I needed to do and she is asleep in the back room," Big Mike comments joining them in Janessa's office.

"What did you give her?" Malcolm inquires.

"Just a little bit of morphine, she'll feel better once she comes to."

Suddenly, a dazed and disheveled Nikki appears in the doorway of Janessa's office. The room goes silent.

"I guess I didn't give her enough." Big Mike murmurs.

"Why were you yelling?" Nikki asks Malcolm.

"How are you feeling?" Malcolm asks.

"Not so good. I have a crazy headache."

" I'll take you home." Malcolm says.

"Okay, thanks," she agrees, too drowsy to argue.

When they hear the front door, close and are sure that they have left, Janessa finally says something.

"What the hell just happened?" she asks Vick and Mike.

"I'm not sure," Vick says.

"So what now?" Mike asks.

"Nothing, we wait," Vick answers.

Nikki and Malcolm ride in his Mercedes to her home in the county. Malcolm usually plays his music loudly, but he has turned it off for Nikki. Nikki is mute.

"Why are you taking me home?" she asks.

"What do you mean?"

"Just a few hours ago you accused me of lying to you and then you let Mike drug me. So why are you taking me home?"

"My head is spinning. I don't know what to think baby girl. You've always been there for me and the things they are saying about you just don't make sense."

"Exactly!" Nikki yells. Nikki grabs her head as pain shoots through it and she begins to massage the middle of her forehead.

"Baby, you got to calm down. You're going to send yourself to the emergency room."

"Calm down? Are you really telling me to calm down?" Nikki begins to raise her voice again.

"Just tell me the truth. No matter what it is, we can work through it." Malcolm tells her calmly.

"Fine, you want the truth. The truth is I didn't say the things Janessa said I did. But...I have been stealing money from you Malcolm, that's the truth."

They pull into the driveway of Nikki's house. Malcolm stares out the window.

"If you needed money, all you had to do was ask and I would have given it to you tenfold." he indicates.

"Look I did five years in prison for you! Why should I have to ask for anything! You're being so stupid Malcolm. Can't you see that Janessa is playing you?"

"Janessa is the one playing me? You just admitted to stealing from me! Me of all people! Let's talk about this more inside," Malcolm says.

"What more is there to say Malcolm?" Nikki replies.

"There's more, there's definitely more, let's go."

Malcolm gets out of the car and waits for Nikki to exit. Nikki gets out of the passenger side and they walk up her grey cobblestone driveway. Nikki opens the door and walks in ahead of Malcolm. Malcolm reaches behind his back. Nikki doesn't turn around. With her back to him she begins to speak.

"So what else is it you want to say?" Nikki asks.

"I just wanted to say goodbye," Malcolm says coldly.

There is a loud pop and then silence.

Janessa, Vick and Mike are back at the office wrapping things up for the day.

"So, you sure he won't hurt her?" Janessa asks Vick.

"I'm sure. Nikki is the love of his life."

"Even after she makes that "confession" about the money?" Janessa asks.

"Yes, I'm sure. It will just make him have another breakdown, which is what we want to happen. Besides, there's no turning back, we've already got the ball rolling."

Mike rushes into the office.

"I got a call from Malcolm. He said he coming back to the office."

"And?" Vick asks.

"And what?" Mike replies.

"How did he sound? Did he say anything about Nikki?" Janessa asks worried.

"Nothing, and he sounded in a good mood actually," Mike says.

Vick takes out his cell phone and calls someone. Sweat beads form on his nose and his breathing speeds up. He hangs up and dials again and again.

"Damn, she's not answering!"

"I knew it, I knew it. He killed her!" Janessa screams.

"Chill. He didn't kill her!" Vick states matter-of-factly trying to calm Janessa down.

"How can you be sure?"

Vick appears unaware of his environment and is repeatedly checking his phone.

"Look man, you have to go by there and check on her." Vick says to Mike.

"Aright man, I'll go now."

"Call me as soon as she answers the door. She's probably in the shower or something."

"Got it," Mike makes haste out of office.

Janessa shudders.

"Babe, it's okay there's no way he would hurt her," Vick tries to reassure her.

"I can hear it in your voice. You're not sure." Janessa starts to cry. "This is going all wrong, I knew it couldn't be this easy."

"Calm down, babe. It will still work. I promise." The pit of her stomach falls.

At last, Vick's phone rings.

"Hello Nikki!"

"Naw, man it's me and things don't look good," Mike's concerned voice comes through the phone.

"What you mean?"

"I'm down the street from the house, but I can't get to the house because it's surrounded by police."

"Fuck!" Vick shouts.

"Okay, I'll get on the radio and see what's going on, just come back to the office."

Vick goes over to his radio that he uses to monitor police activity in the area. He plays with the knobs until he hears what he is looking for. A man can be heard over static "we need someone from the coroner's office to come to 816 Fort Ave".

"That's Nikki's address!" Janessa shrieks.

Malcolm strolls into the office.

"Hey guys, what's going on?" he says casually.

Janessa stares at the floor afraid to look at Malcolm. Vick makes quick strides over to him and gets right in his face.

"What the hell did you do man?"

"I'm not sure what your problem is, but you got five seconds to get the fuck out of my face."

Malcolm and Vick maintain the stare off, each waiting for the other to back down first. Finally, Vick backs off.

"Where's Nikki?" Vick asks.

"At home where I dropped her off I guess." Malcolm answers not hinting at what just happened. "Why? You know something I don't?"

"Man stop fucking with me. Mike just called me from her house. It's surrounded by cops and the scanner is saying they need someone from the coroner's office to come to the house," Vick challenges him.

"I did what was necessary."

"You did what was necessary? She's been down with you since the very beginning," Vick says in disbelief.

"I finally put two and two together. She was the leak. She had to have been the one feeding the authorities information. I knew something was up the minute she got out of jail. I've been planning for a while to get rid of her, but I didn't have the heart, until she told she was stealing from me. Then it was easy."

"You're lying, you're lying!" Vick hollers.

With a slow steady gait, Malcolm strides over to the coffee maker and begins to make himself a cup. Janessa is unable to think as a sudden coldness hits her core.

"Well, let's get to work. This money isn't going to be made by itself," Malcolm says, waiving his cup of coffee.

With a smirk on his face he saunters out of the office.

"Is he for real?" Janessa asks Vick.

"I think he is, but we can still fix this."

"Are you serious? You can't really want to continue this."

Vick grabs Janessa by the shoulders and begins to shake her violently

"Look, this needs to happen," he shouts.

Fear splinters in her heart. She nods her head yes. He releases his scrunched-up face and begins to talk with composure.

"I'm sorry, I didn't mean to scare you, but I have a lot more at stake then you will ever know and this plan has to work."

"So now what, now that she's gone?" Janessa asks hesitantly.

"I got to think about that. But I'll have something for us by tomorrow."

"So soon?"

"We got to move quick. He is becoming unstable quicker than I anticipated."

Mike creeps into the room. Tears shone in his eyes.

"I can't believe this is happening. Since when do we take out our own," Mike mourns.

"He lost it again," Vick answers trying to hide any involvement.

"But Nikki? Of all people, Nikki? This shit doesn't make any sense. Look I got to get out of here for the day. I'm out."

Mike begins to approach the door, but then Malcolm appears out of nowhere.

"Where the hell do you think you're going?" he asks with authority.

"Yo, chill man. You might not have an issue with taking out someone you were supposed to love, but I do," Mike stands his ground.

"Oh so now you take issue with how I run things around here?"

"Hell yes! She's been part of the family since the beginning. You have really lost your mind this time."

Malcolm's eyes widen, showing the whites. He pulls a gun from his waistband and points the black metal barrel in Mike's face.

"Are you calling me crazy?" he demands.

Mike fearlessly thrust out his chest.

"Who's the one pointing a gun at one of their best friends?" Mike asks.

Malcolm inches forward. He begins to squeeze the trigger. Mike crosses his arms in front of his chest. Vick and Janessa watch, helpless to intervene. At last, Malcolm releases his finger from the trigger, puts the gun down by his side and walks out. A splash of fluid hits the floor and it takes Janessa a few seconds to realize that she threw up. She closes her eyes and begins to pray. Mike marches by her.

"I think you're going to need a lot more than prayer to come out this one alive." says Mike.

She opens her eyes just in time to watch Mike disappear out the office. She stares down at the liquid mess she made on the fancy carpet. There is a deafening silence in the room as she continues to stare at her vomit on the floor.

"You should clean that up and then go home," Vick says.

"Yeah, sure," she whispers.

As she drives home, Janessa doesn't remember cleaning up the mess, just the smell of carpet cleaner and air freshener. It's like she is having mini blackouts. She wants out, and she wants out now. She can't trust anyone. Not even Vick. Her eyes are completely open to the fact that there is no loyalty or love in this business and it's every man or woman for themselves. She should come up with her own exit strategy and if she comes out unharmed that is all the matters. Janessa is so exhausted that the blue lights on her radio seem to be dancing around. As she drives up her winding driveway, she begins to think about Nikki. She wonders if she suffered, if she knew it was Malcolm that ended her life, and if she did know how did she feel? Despite Nikki's flaws Janessa would have never wished that kind of death on her.

Surely if he could do that to his lover and friend of more than twenty years, he would snuff out Janessa without hesitation. She begins to wonder if that is not his next course of action. Why wouldn't he kill her? Question after question runs through her head. She sits in her idling car and images of what Nikki's body might have looked like after he killed her haunt Janessa's thoughts. She is startled out of her trance by the ringing of her cell phone through the car's blue tooth connection. The caller ID announces that it's Demetrius on the line. Janessa bursts into tears, but can calm herself enough to answer the phone.

"What's going on babe? I haven't heard from you all day," Demetrius says. Janessa can hear the concern in his voice.

"Long day. Can you please come over?"

"I have to go to work in four hours. I was going to try to get some sleep."

"Oh, okay," Janessa stammers.

"Everything okay? I can come over if you really need me to."

Janessa can no longer hold back her tears and begins to sob uncontrollably.

"Yes, I really need you . Please come now."

"Baby, baby. What happened? Tell me now!"

"I can't. I have to speak to you in person."

"I'll be there in a few minutes. I'm going to use my lights," he says with authority.

"Please hurry."

She continues to cry uncontrollably. Tears pour down her cheeks, soaking the collar of her $500 blouse. Her eyes quickly swell and she has no choice but to close them. She can hear sirens off in the distance and she knows it's Demetrius. Even with her eyes closed she can see the blue and red flashing lights pull up behind her BMW. Before she knows it, Demetrius is sitting next to her in the passenger side of her car.

"What happened baby? Please tell me!"

"Demetrius…I don't even know where to start. It's horrible and I'm next if I don't get out." Janessa trembles fighting back more tears.

"Next? Janessa what the hell is going on!"

Janessa's face glistens with sweat and her eyes dart wildly from side to side.

"He killed her and I'm next!" Janessa says frantically.

Demetrius grabs her gently by the shoulders and moves a piece of hair stuck to the lip gloss on her lips.

"Baby, Calm down. You're not making any sense. Who killed who? And why are you next?"

It's then she realizes that Demetrius has no idea what she has been up to for a year. She takes several deep breaths to calm her nerves. After regaining her composure, she begins to recount what's been her life the past year; the blackmail, the greed, and the murder that has unfolded. Demetrius lowers his head unable to look Janessa in the eye.

"I can't believe what you're telling me," he finally musters.

"Just hearing myself say it, I honestly can't believe it either."

She puts her face into her hands, ashamed that Demetrius' opinion of her has now inevitably changed.

"I knew something was up."

"Something like what? And why?" she asks.

"Call it cop's institution, but ever since I saw you with Malcolm that day, I just knew something wasn't right. It made no sense why he would hire you to be his lawyer. Besides you never represented him at his trial. It was that big time Jewish attorney William Friedman."

"Yeah, well I was supposed to represent him in that case...but clearly I was busy with other things, and why is it so unbelievable that he would choose me as his attorney?"

"You ever considered that this was a set up from the moment he walked into your office asking for representation. I'm telling you I know this man. He does nothing by accident." implores Demetrius.

Janessa contemplates what Demetrius just said to her. She reflects on the day Malcolm asked her to represent him. She remembers how shocked people were when she told them who had popped into her office asking for representation. She can still smell the fresh stack of money he dropped on her desk. The bills were so straight and crisp. She had never seen that much money at one time before. Malcolm with his charming smile as he assured it was all there, $25,000. She hadn't even told him how much it would cost to represent him but there was no way she was going to turn down that kind of money. The sky has gotten dark, pitch black almost.

"A set up huh." she says.

"Yeah, a set-up."

"A set up for what?" she asks.

"That I don't know. But what I can promise you is that you're in a lot of danger, especially if it's true that he killed Nikki." he says.

"You know how important she was to him?"

"Like I said before, I've arrested this man many times. I know a lot about him and the people he affiliates with."

Janessa starts to wonder if he knows about Vick and Big Mike too.

"Will you help me?" asks Janessa.

"Of course baby. I love you and I want to finally see Malcolm go down forever."

"Do you know much about his partner Vick?"

"Oh is he still is working with him huh? They've been together for years. He's not to be trusted either." warns Demetrius.

"Really, Vick?" says Janessa.

"Yeah Vick. Why? Ya'll BFFs now or possibly more? He's known to mess with anything with a vagina."

Janessa pretends as though she is not hurt by Demetrius' statement.

"I could see that." she utters.

"I got to get to work soon. But I'll get you out of this. I promise ."

Janessa can feel his brown eyes piercing hers despite the darkness. She turns on the overhead light and begins to admire his handsome face. His goatee fits his face perfectly. He has a small piece of white lint right above his lower lip. She gently wipes it off.

"What I got a booger?" he jokes.

They laugh in unison.

"No babe. Just a piece of lint. You really promise?"

"I promise. I will get you out of this and they will go down."

She leans and begins to passionately kiss him.

"I love you." Janessa whispers in his ear.

He smiles and pecks her on the cheek.

"I have to go but I will call you right after roll call ."

"Okay babe."

He jumps out the car, gets back into his squad car and skirts off into the night. It felt so good to finally tell someone about everything. Fifty pounds has been lifted from her chest and the oxygen flows easily through her lungs. Feelings of security, love and hopefulness overwhelm her body. It's finally going to come to an end and she can be free of Malcolm and Vick!

TEN

The next day when her alarm goes off Janessa eagerly leaps out of her bed. Demetrius should be getting off work now. She can't wait to call him, her knight in shining armor. All night she had dreams about him, dreams of him bursting into her office, arresting Malcolm and Vick and taking them away from her life forever. She sings loudly in the shower. As she is stepping out of the shower her phone rings but it's not her knight in shining armor as she had hoped but her puppet master, Malcolm. She lets it go to voicemail, knowing very well he is going to call right back.

Sure, enough only a few seconds later her phone rings again.

"Good morning Mr. Jacobs." she answers.

"Good morning Ms. Nikolas."

"What can I do for you boss?" she asks.

"Well…you can meet me at my home around 12pm."

"Your home?" Janessa says fearfully.

It has been almost a year and she had never been to Malcolm or Vick's home. She figured they kept that part of their life private for a reason. A sickening feeling overwhelms Janessa. Why would he invite her to his home now? Something isn't right and she knows it. She longs for Demetrius. She can't tell if her shakes are because of the cold air hitting her wet body or from fear. "Yes my home. Well at least one of them." he replies

"Why?" asks Janessa.

"Why? Because I asked you to, that's why."

"I'm sorry. You said 12pm, correct" she gulps.

"Yep. I'll send a car for you." instructs Malcolm.

"I can drive."

"No. I will send a car. It will be at your house by 11:15am."

"Yes sir."

She hangs up the phone still shaking and immediately begins to dial Demetrius. As she is about to hit the call button Demetrius is calling her.

"Baby he asked me to come to his home!" she shrieks.

"Who?" asks Demetrius.

"Malcolm!"

"Is that unusual?"

"Yes! I've never been there before. I have no idea where he lives. I'm scared!"

"Baby, baby. Calm down. He won't hurt you." says Demetrius calmly.

"How do you know?" asks Janessa.

"Because I know him like the back of my hand. He wouldn't hurt someone who is making him money. That is the only thing that motivates him. You'll be fine."

"But...Nikki was making money for him and why now after all this time would he ask me to his home?"

"Nikki did the one thing that would get her killed, which would be to betray Malcolm. But I am certain the reason he asked you to his home is because he trust you. This is perfect." exclaims Demetrius.

"How do you know what she did to get herself killed?"

"Huh? Ummm...I don't know, that would be my best guess though. You want him to go down right?" Demetrius quickly changes the subject.

"Yes more than ever!" responds Janessa.

"Then you need to find out as much information as possible."

"What kind of information? Don't I know enough already?"

"Are you sure? What do you know?" asks Demetrius.

"Um…I know…um..."

"Exactly. You don't know anything. You don't know who supplies his drugs, you don't know who else works for him. You don't know how many cities he sells in. You don't know how many cops he has on his payroll. You don't know how much money he is making. You don't know who and how he transports his drugs. You don't know squat." says Demetrius.

"Oh."

He's right. Janessa can't believe she has worked for this man for this long and literally knows nothing. Not even where the man lives. How is that possible? She's been nothing but his puppet. Doing as told and never asking questions. Wow, how did she become this person? She sits down on her bed wrapped in a towel letting Demetrius' truth soak in.

"You need to find that stuff out. That's the only way he is finally going down for good." says Demetrius.

"If I haven't gotten any of that information up until this point, how do you suppose I get it now?"

"That's because you weren't looking for it. I'm sure you were blindly doing as you were told since they had the theft hanging over your head. But today none of that matters because you have me in your corner and I promise you, I won't let you fall." insists Demetrius.

"What if he becomes suspicious? Then he will definitely kill me." Janessa announces.

"You're a smart girl. The fact that you survived those two this long speaks to that."

"Really?"

"Yes definitely. Look I need to get some rest, but I'll be over later tonight and we will talk details. Trust me it's all going to work out.

"Love you."

"Love you too."

She starts to dry off but there is no need as her skin has air-dried. Her anxiety is on high, as she gets ready to meet with Malcolm at his home. She decides on a dressy, but casual look. She keeps checking herself in the mirror wondering if Malcolm would notice anything different about her. She looked as she always did on the outside but she certainly didn't feel like the same person on the inside. She didn't want this new feeling of strength and confidence to reveal itself on the outside and tip Malcolm off that she was up to something.

She hears the dog walker, Andy downstairs getting Truth and Justice ready for their daily trip to the dog park. They must be some of the most spoiled dogs on the planet Janessa thinks to herself. She takes one more look at herself in the mirror and goes downstairs to make herself some coffee. By now it's 10:30a.m. giving her about 45 minutes to relax. She throws her head back as she takes in the fresh coffee aroma. While simultaneously sipping her coffee, she acts out what she will do and say when she is at Malcolm's house. She is in the middle of having a pretend conversation with Malcolm when Andy comes back with Truth and Justice.

Luckily Andy doesn't notice Janessa speaking to herself.

"Were they angels as usual?" she asks Andy.

Andy and Janessa both laugh at the question since they both know Truth and Justice are far from being angels, more like spoiled brats who refuse to listen.

"Oh yeah. Perfect angels as usual." Andy replies with a chuckle.

"See you guys next time. Bye Janessa."

"See you later Andy."

Andy leaves and the dogs run off to their playroom. She finishes her coffee and sits at her bar waiting for Malcolm's car service to pick her up. The antique grandfather clock ticks in slow motion and each tick appears to get louder and louder. 11:05, 11:06…11:11…11:15 finally arrives and at the exact moment the clock strikes 11:15 a black SUV pulls up to Janessa's home. She jumps off the bar stool and hurries outside. A gentleman is already exiting the SUV and circling around to the front passenger side door. It's a familiar face.

"Big Mike!" shouts Janessa.

"Hey sweetheart." says Big Mike.

"Malcolm didn't tell me it was you who was picking me up."

"Well it's me. Is that okay?"

"Yes. It's a relief."

"I feel that. Let's get out of here, don't want to be late." says Big Mike.

"Absolutely."

Janessa pulls herself into the large SUV. She has flashbacks of climbing into Demetrius' pickup truck and him using her bottom as leverage to help her into the truck. The memory brings a smile to her face. Big Mike takes notice.

"What are you so happy about?" he asks.

"Oh nothing." Janessa replies.

"Sure. Have you ever been to one of Malcolm's homes before?"

"No. Never. You?"

"I've known that man for more than ten years and I still haven't been to all of them, but I've been to a couple. He's one of the most private men you will ever meet." says Big Mike.

"I've noticed. What about Vick?" asks Janessa.

"What about Vick? Are you asking me if he's private too, or if he's been to Malcolm's homes?"

"Well both I guess."

A burst of sunlight strikes both Janessa and Big Mike in the eyes. Janessa slides on her $900 shades and Mike pulls down his visor. Mike starts changing the station on the radio from the steering wheel.

"That sound like questions you should be asking Vick."
Janessa lets out an exaggerated sigh. .
"I suppose."
"So are you okay? I know how upset we all were about what happened the other day." she says.
Big Mike turns his face away.
"I hate this song. It's so corny." he says.
"So are you okay?" she repeats.
"No time to talk. We're here."
Janessa hadn't even noticed that they pulled up to large black gate with an equally large gold letter M on the front of it. Big Mike pulls up close to the gate and a robotic voice from the speaker box next to Big Mike's window says "Enter." The slowness for which the gates opens spooks Janessa. She feels like she is entering a haunted house. They drive up a long, driveway and finally arrive at the house. The house is breathtaking. Beautiful flowers that represent all colors of the rainbow surround the property. The trees and the grass are so green and immaculately cut that they look like a painting. Janessa thought her home was impressive but compared to Malcolm's home, it was a shack!
"I felt the same way when I first came here." says Mike.
She is admiring the beauty that surrounds her. The home is much larger than she ever imagined. It reminds her of an updated version of an old mid-century castle. As she continues to take it all in, her breath shakes at the sight of several crows lined up on edge of the roof. They remind her of the crows that were perched outside Malcolm's office the first time she visited. She always believed that their presence was a sign of bad things to come.
"You ready to go in?" asks Big Mike.
"Um give me a second to freshen up." Janessa says.
She pulls down her visor and takes off her sunglasses. She pulls out a small bottle of lotion, lip-gloss and mascara from her purse.
"You do know you're going to see Malcolm, not your man"

"Yes I know, but that doesn't mean I should go in there looking a mess!"

"Fine. I'll be waiting outside."

Big Mike steps out the SUV and stands by the door. Janessa lotions her face and arms, then applies fresh lip-gloss and mascara. She finishes up by spraying a quick squirt of body spray on her chest. She closes her eyes and pictures Demetrius' handsome face. "I'll make you proud babe." she whispers to herself.

She slides out of the SUV and meets Big Mike on the driver's side where he is still standing. He is on the phone. She stares up at the peering crows as she waits for Big Mike to finish his conversation. She shoots at them with her finger gun.

"What did they do to you?" says Big Mike chuckling.

"They keep staring at me!" she proclaims.

"Aw girl, they just nosey that's all."

"Well I don't like it."

"Okay let's get you safe and away from them dangerous crows." says Big Mike mockingly.

Malcolm has already opened the door. Janessa takes several big breaths preparing herself for what may come once she is behind closed doors with Malcolm. She prays that Demetrius is right and she won't end up like Nikki. Sweat forms in the small of her back. In her head, she is telling herself to calm down. She doesn't want to tip Malcolm off to anything. It seems like it takes hours to make it inside the home where Malcolm is standing in the foyer waiting for them.

"Aright man. Thanks for driving. You can go and I'll call you when she's ready to go home." Malcolm says to Big Mike.

Janessa is relieved to hear that Malcolm has plans for her to return home tonight.

"Man I gotta drive back here. You know I live almost an hour from here." Big Mike replies.

"Man up and stop whining! I pay you enough fucking money

for you not to be tripping about driving an hour somewhere." yells Malcolm.

"My bad man. You right. Just hit me up when you're ready for her to be picked up."

"That's better." Malcolm says.

Big Mike leaves Janessa and Malcolm alone.

"So welcome to my humble home!" chimes Malcolm.

"Yeah sure humble." she laughs.

"Well humble for me at least. Let's go into the study."

Janessa follows closely behind him. She is trying her best to control her breathing and sweating. They seem to walk in circles for several seconds before reaching the study. It's dark and musky. Malcolm says lights and it brightens. There are at least five computer monitors circling a long brown desk. It reminds her of something she's seen in a movie about a stockbroker.

"Something to drink?" Malcolm asks.

"Water." she responds.

"That's it?"

"I'll take a lemon too."

"Sure no problem."

He pushes a button on the desk and speaks.

"Water with freshly sliced lemon and Vodka on the rocks."

"Yes sir. Right away." says a woman on the other end.

"Oh my bad did you want something to eat with your lemon water?" he asks.

"No thanks. I'm fine."

"You want to know why the hell you're here right?"

"That would be nice." she says.

"I wanted to speak with you personally about what went down with Nikki."

The mention of Nikki's name makes her blood run cold and her flesh prickle.

"Sit down. You look like you're going to faint." says Malcolm.

As Malcolm helps her into a cushy, tan leather chair a young woman walks into the room with the drinks.

"Everything okay sir?" she asks.

"Yeah fine. Perfect timing with the water."

She hands Janessa a wine glass filled with water and finely sliced lemon dancing about the glass. It almost looked to pretty to drink.

"Sip that. You'll feel better. Sherri here makes the best lemon water around." he says.

The young woman blushes.

"Anything else sir?" Sherri asks Malcolm.

"Nothing for now. But we may want something to eat later."

"Okay sir. Just ring me with your orders when you're ready and I'll be sure the chef prepares whatever you need."

"Great thanks."

Before Sherri exits the study, Malcolm grabs her and overpoweringly kisses her. Sherri's arms remain by her side. Janessa lowers her eyes and chews on her cuticle. Malcolm gropes and kisses Sherri for several seconds unbothered by Janessa's presence. They ultimately finish and she scurries out of the office.

"Is the water helping?" he asks Janessa.

"Oh um I haven't drank any yet."

"Drink, drink. You'll feel better right away." says Malcolm.

She does as she is instructed and begins to drink the water.

"Not to fast now. Sip it slowly."

He walks over to where Janessa sits, holds the glass for her and brings it to her lips. She takes as small sips as she physically can. She is afraid that if she doesn't he will get angry. Malcolm gently holds the back of her neck while he uses his other hand to hold the glass to Janessa's lips. She feels like child learning how to drink from a grown-up cup for the first time.

"Feel better?"

"Yes much better." she fibs.

"I understand why you would get frightened hearing Nikki's name. But that is why I want to explain things to you myself. Face to face. And the reason I invited you to my home is because I wanted to show you how much trust I have in you now."

"Thanks." says Janessa in between another sip of water.

"Aright so where do I start. You know Nikki was my everything. When I was a nobody making a few dollars dealing dime bags on the corner, she was by my side and from then on she never left. I'm sure you've learned that it's almost impossible to keep loyal friends in this business."

"Yes I've noticed." Janessa says.

"I thought she would always be down for me especially after she did time for me, so when I found out what she was doing behind my back it almost broke me."

"What she was doing?" she asks

"Yes. She was working for the other side." claims Malcolm.

Janessa's heart skips a beat.

"The police?"

"No. She was working with Karl."

"Whose Karl?"

"He has been trying to take over my enterprise for years. Karl got me started in this game. Honestly taught me everything I know. It should have been both of us running this thing together, but he committed the ultimate betrayal by becoming a snitch for the Feds and ever since then we've been enemies."

"Did he get you locked up?"

"Nah. Even so, he did get a lot of others locked up and that I could never forgive." Malcolm says.

"So how did you find out she was working with Karl?"

"It doesn't matter. All that matters is that I found out. Bottom line she is gone and now you need to step up."

Janessa is attempting to comprehend what Malcolm has told her since she believed he had killed Nikki after she told Malcolm the story about the money that Vick had conjured up.

"Step up?" Janessa asks.

"Yeah I can trust you. I know you didn't do this in the beginning because you wanted to, but I've seen a change in you over the last year. I know now you're in this not just to save yourself but because you want to be here." assumes Malcolm.

Janessa begins to think about what Demetrius said. To get Malcolm's trust so Demetrius can finally take him down for good. Malcolm was completely wrong in his assessment of Janessa. She is still only working for him because she feels she should, although she did have her moments where she forgot that. Nonetheless she wanted out.

Sherri peeks back into the room. Malcolm waives her off.

"Am I right?" Malcolm asks Janessa.

"I didn't think you noticed." Janessa replies.

"I notice everything. Now that I know I can trust you completely, the real work can begin."

"I'm ready."

ELEVEN

Before she can digest what Malcolm has said to her, she is back in the SUV with Big Mike on her way home. The sky is a grey-blue color. As they ride along the beltway Janessa feels like she is floating in a spaceship. Her conversation with Malcolm was both intriguing and terrifying. He wants her to replace Nikki. She could never replace Nikki. She wouldn't do the things Nikki did for him, especially go to jail.

"So how did it go?" Big Mike asks Janessa.

"Um well I guess."

"So...what did he want?" implores Big Mike.

"He wanted my help."

"Your help?"

"Yes my help. Hey is that woman his wife?" asks Janessa.

"Wife! Yeah right." Big Mike bellows.

"Girlfriend?"

"Nah no girlfriend, no wife. Why? What happened?" he asks.

"I don't know how to explain it really...it was just."

"You don't have to tell me. I know. He takes what he wants, when he wants it. You be careful not to forget what he really is." says Big Mike.

"What's that?" she asks.

"The devil himself."

The sun rises and Janessa emerges from her bedroom to make breakfast for herself and Demetrius. After telling Demetrius everything that happened at Malcolm's house he is more than sure that they will be able to bring down Malcolm for good and soon too. Janessa is ecstatic to hear the news and prays that Demetrius is right. She can hear the dogs eagerly waiting by the door for their morning walk with Andy. Janessa is so grateful she can afford luxuries such as a dog walker. As the coffee brews her cell phone goes off. Before she even looks at the caller ID she already knows who it is. It's her mother; she forgot to call her last night as promised. Janessa has been a horrible daughter, sister and friend the last few months. She can only hope that one day she will be able to explain to them why she was distant and ask for their forgiveness.

"Good morning mom. I'm so sorry I didn't call you last night as promised."

"Honey. I don't understand what has been going on with you lately. I used to hear from you weekly now I barely hear from you on a monthly basis." implores her mom.

"I know. I feel horrible."

"You know money will never be able to replace the unconditional love of your family."

"I understand mom."

Janessa unexpectedly begins to tear up. She changes the subject.

"So are you excited for your trip to Hawaii? This is your first time, right?" asks Janessa

"Yes. I'm excited. I went bathing suit shopping yesterday, found a couple that are suitable for an old lady like myself." Janessa chuckles.

"Please mom. You're still a hot mama!"

"Well thank you dear I appreciate that. Other than work how are things? You do have a life outside of work correct?" Janessa's mother asks.

"Yes mommy. I've met someone. It has gotten serious. I can't wait for you and Angel to meet him."

"Oh really. Well that's some good news. I'm glad to know that someone gets to spend time with you other than your Partners."

Janessa could no longer avoid speaking about Malcolm and Vick so she told her mother and her sister that Malcolm and Vick were silent Partners that had invested into her firm so that she could stay in business.

"Things are going to change real soon mom and you will be hearing from me and seeing me more than you can take. I promise!" says Janessa.

"Oh yeah what kind of changes?" her mother asks.

"I can't really get into details right now. But soon is all I can say."

"Well okay. I truly hope so. I miss you."

Again, the tears begin to form in Janessa's brown eyes.

"I miss you too. I must get ready for work. I love you and I will call you later this week."

"Love you too."

Janessa wipes the moisture from her eyes with the collar of Demetrius t-shirt that she wore to bed. She has just finished drying her eyes when Demetrius saunters into the kitchen. His curly hair is frizzed and he still has crust in his eyes. He shuffles over to Janessa, gives her a peck on the cheek, sits at the bar and turns on the television.

"Sleep well?" Janessa asks.

"Absolutely. Especially after that news you gave me last night. I can't wait to take him down." responds Demetrius.

"So is this mission about rescuing me or taking down Malcolm?"

Demetrius has become emerged in a story on Sports Center and doesn't respond.

"I'm sorry babe. What did you say?" he asks.

"It seems that you are more concerned with taking Malcolm down than you are about rescuing me. Which is more important to you?"

He rolls his shoulders, hops off the bar stool and engulfs Janessa in a big bear hug.

"Babe of course rescuing you is more important. I'm sorry if it doesn't seem that way. I love you very much and wouldn't want anything bad to happen to you."

He releases her from the hold of his muscular, tattooed arms.

"I love you too." she mumbles.

It's nearly afternoon and Demetrius has left to go home and get ready for his shift later that night. Janessa paces her bedroom. Feelings of unrest hover over her. She didn't believe a word of what Demetrius said when he claimed this mission was about her. Is he using her? Does he love her? Maybe he knew all along what she was doing and was waiting for her to come clean so he could come to her "rescue". Or worst he is working for Malcolm and Vick too! Her phone rings. She is happy to see that it is Vick.

"Hey." says Janessa.

"So taking the day off huh?"

"No. Just a late start that's all." she replies.

"Right. So how late is a late start?" he asks.

"I'll be there by 3 o' clock."

"Fine. I'll be there when you get there." Vick says.

As promised Janessa arrives at the office at 3 o' clock on the dot. Vick is not there as he promised. She hasn't seen Vick in at least three weeks. Even though she hasn't said anything about dating a cop she is certain that both Vick and Malcolm know all about it. She imagined that they would be extremely upset to find out she was dating a Baltimore City cop, but they haven't said a word which is both good news and worrisome at the same time. But Janessa was certain Demetrius could handle himself; it was herself she was most concerned about. Janessa is making coffee when Vick barges into the office. His hair is in a mini afro not close cut like he usually wears it and his facial hair has grown in weird patches around his face. Janessa is shocked to see him looking so rugged.

"What's up?" he asks Janessa. "Nothing. You okay?"

"Yeah why?" asks Vick.

He gets a glimpse of his reflection in one of the paintings on the wall.

"Oh this" he points to his face. "My friend was in the hospital for a week. I didn't have time to do anything with myself."

"Sorry to hear that. Are they going to be okay?" asks Janessa.

"Yeah doctors say she is going to be okay. You don't want to know?" asks Vick.

"Know what?"

"Who I am talking about." says Vick.

"Not really. Your personal business is certainly no business of mine." Janessa affirms.

Vick gives a mirthless laugh and leans against the wall.

" So...how's business?"

"Going well. It looks like this month is going to exceed expectations as usual."

"Great."

Janessa sips her coffee and goes to her desk. Vick begins to pick out his afro in the reflection of the painting on the wall.

"Did you need something Vick?"

"Do I need something? Why you ask that?"

"On the phone earlier it sounded like you needed something and that is why you wanted to meet me at the office." Janessa reminds him.

He inches over to Janessa's desk and begins to massage her shoulders. She cringes. Vick begins to massage even harder.

"Ouch!" she shrieks.

"What's wrong baby? I thought you liked it rough." he asserts.

"What the hell is wrong with you?" yells Janessa.

He finally lets up and hastily spins her chair around. Her legs are now facing him. His body comes to attention and he takes off his belt. Janessa springs from the chair but Vick violently shoves her back down. Her heart thumps.

"What the fuck is your problem?" cries Janessa.

He doesn't say a word and tries to fondle Janessa's breast. She smacks his hand away and gives him a swift, hard kick to his shin. He buckles briefly from the pain, allowing Janessa to jump to her feet and runs to the front door. As she enters the hallway she runs smack into Malcolm.

"Hey, hey. What's going on? Are we being robbed?" Malcolm frantically asks.

"No. It's Vick! He's lost it!" she says in between sobs.

"What?"

Malcolm rushes into the office. She can hear scuffling from behind the closed door. The window is tinted a dark black so she cannot see what is going on. She hears yelling mostly from Malcolm. She reaches for her cell phone to call Demetrius but she left it on her desk inside the office. The yelling and scuffling has stopped and Janessa can't hear anything. She presses her ear against the tinted door. She thinks she hears someone crying. Abruptly the door swings open and Janessa falls into the office. Embarrassed she quickly lifts herself off the floor and Malcolm asks her if she's okay.

"I'm fine. Thanks." she responds.

"Good. Vick has something he needs to say to you."

Vick treads toward Janessa. She takes a couple steps backwards toward the open door behind her.

"I'm not going to touch you . I'm sorry. My behavior toward you was deplorable and it will never happen again." concedes Vick.

Janessa can see the tear stains on his face. His eyes look empty and sad. She wishes that Malcolm hadn't gotten involved and they could have resolved it themselves.

"Thanks I appreciate the apology and I accept. But what's

going on? Why...?"

"The whys don't matter. What matters is that it won't happen again." booms Malcolm.

"I gotta go. Again, I'm very sorry Janessa." whimpers Vick.

Vick dashes out of the office. Janessa stares down at the beautiful red and white carpet beneath her feet, her shoulders sagged. When she lifts her head, she is reminded that Malcolm is still there. He is sitting at her desk nonchalantly going through some papers. Compared to the way Vick looked, Malcolm looks like a top model. His hair is cut low and nicely edged up. His beard is neatly shaped to his face and his dark suit looks impeccable especially with the orange and blue tie to compliment it. Malcolm motions for Janessa to sit. She drags her feet over to the desk and sits in the chair across from him.

"We tried to warn you." taunts Malcolm.

"Who's we? And tried to warn me about what?" "Nikki and I tried to warn you about Vick."

"I don't recall any warnings." scoffs Janessa.

She finds it especially odd that a man as dangerous as Malcolm would be warning her about Vick.

"Fine. If you say so." says Malcolm without looking up from the paperwork.

"Is he going to be okay? What's going on with him?" she asks.

"That's not my place to say. Don't worry though when I say that will never happen again I mean it. It won't happen again." says Malcolm finally looking up from the paperwork.

Janessa is itching to know more but knows there is no use in trying to get any information from Malcolm.

"Okay. Thanks for the help."

"Of course. We're a team, right?" asks Malcolm.

"Yes." she wilted.

"Soon it will just be us and then we'll take this business to the next level."

"Vick's leaving?" she questions.

"Yeah you could say that."

Her chest caves and she excuses herself from the office and makes her way to the bathroom. She stares in the mirror. She doesn't recognize the woman that stares back at her. The eyes that once reflected hope and life are now vacant, nothing but black dots. She can't remember what her smile looks like anymore because she rarely gets to use it. The constant crying seems to have left her eyes permanently puffy.

"Hey you okay in there?" Malcolm shouts through the closed bathroom door.

"Oh yeah. I'll be right out."

"Okay I need to head out. I'll call you later okay."

She steps out of the bathroom.

"Okay. I'll talk to you later."

Malcolm puts his large, calloused hand on her shoulder. She bows her head.

"Pack up, go home and get some rest. As a matter of fact, take the week. I'll take care of business." Malcolm says.

"Really? Thanks. I could use the break."

"I agree especially with the changes that are coming."

"Changes?" Janessa echoes.

"Don't worry about it. We'll talk when you get back from your R & R aright."

"Aright."

Screeching tires penetrate the air as Janessa's BMW swerves in and out of traffic. She is hopeful that Demetrius is already at her place. She texted him to let him know she had the week off and that she needed him by her side tonight. However, she is disappointed when she pulls up and his car is not there. She checks her phone for a text message, but nothing. "Damn he must be pulling overtime" Janessa says to herself.

She creeps up her long, winding driveway anticipating that she will see the familiar sight of blue headlights pulling up behind her. Sadness consumes her when she reaches the top of her driveway and Demetrius is still not there. She drags herself into the house. Her dogs Truth and Justice come charging out of their bedroom excited to see their mom home so early. She musters up a little bit of strength to greet them.

Janessa aimlessly roams around her home anxiously waiting for Demetrius to call her back. Her drawstring less, pink and black flower print pajama pants keep falling off. Truth and Justice pace back and forth with her in the kitchen. Eventually, the lovely sound of the ring tone she assigned to Demetrius can be heard echoing throughout the kitchen.

"Babe!" says Janessa as she answers her phone.

"Hey babe, what's up? You okay?" he asks.

"Well yes and no. I really need to talk to you, can you come over tonight?"

"Yeah of course. I'll be there in an hour." Demetrius responds.

"Ok. See you then."

Janessa fumbles around the kitchen in anticipation of telling Demetrius what happened with Vick. Demetrius arrives an hour later. She rushes to the door to greet him tripping on her pants on the way. A rush of warm air hits her in the face as she opens the door. She embraces him with a hug and his strong arms squeeze tight around her . As she crumbles in his arms she forgets all about the incident with Vick

"What do I owe the pleasure of such an ecstatic greeting?" he asks.

"I miss you and love you. That's why."

"I love you too baby. Are you going to let me in the house now?" he chuckles.

"Oh sorry."

She moves out of the way so he can get into the house. Now it's Truth and Justice turn to greet him. The two four-legged bundles of black fur jump up and down with excitement. He gives them his typical rough housing greeting, which they thoroughly enjoy. She hurries to the kitchen to grab Demetrius his favorite beer out of the refrigerator. She hands him the cold beer in the family room where he is already watching the sports channel.

"Thanks babe." he says.

"Welcome."

She cuddles up next him on the loveseat and he puts his arm over her shoulder.

"Ouch." she says.

"What's the matter?"

Demetrius pulls her t-shirt back enough to look at her neck.

"You have a bruise." he says curiously.

Without warning she is struck with the memory of what Vick tried to do to her earlier that day.

"Yeah about that. Babe you won't believe what happened to me today."

He takes a large swig of his beer all while still looking at the television and then turns to Janessa.

"What? Malcolm confessed all his crimes and you have it all on video." he jokes.

"No this is serious. It…it was Vick."

"Vick confessed all his crimes?" asks Demetrius.

"No. He attacked me."

"What!" shouts Demetrius.

Janessa waits for the ringing to dissipate in her ears before she begins to speak.

"Babe it was awful. It was like he was in some kind of trance."

"When did this happen? And what do you mean attack?" he huffs.

She focuses on the Demetrius flaring nostrils as she talks.

"It was this afternoon in the office. He tried to have sex with me against my will…I think."

"You think?"

"Well I mean he definitely tried to touch me without my permission. I don't know if he would have taken it as far as raping me. I doubt it."

"Why do you doubt it? It's not like you guys have ever had sex before."

Silence. Demetrius hands squeeze into a fist and he cocks his head to the right.

"You guys haven't, right?" he asks through clinched teeth.

Janessa still doesn't answer. Perspiration forms on her lower lip and her throat dries up like the Sahara desert. He unclenches his fist and his breath quickens. Demetrius pulls his face close to hers and asks again. She concentrates on the beer smell tickling her nose hairs.

"Did you and Vick have a sexual relationship?"

"It was a long time ago. I was lonely and vulnerable and he took advantage of that." she insists.

"BULLSHIT!" roars Demetrius even louder than the last time.

She avoids his stare and perspiration is also forming on her cheeks and forehead. She flinches as Demetrius raises himself off the couch. He begins to pace the room mumbling to himself. Janessa can only sit there and watch nervously waiting for him to speak to her. But he doesn't say anything else to her and he leaves the family room. She jumps at each slamming door that rings throughout the house. She can hear Truth and Justice whimpering. Tears fall from her eyes. The one ally she had, is now seemingly her enemy. Demetrius finally comes storming back into the family room with an arm full of clothing.

"You thought you were going to fucking play me!"

"What?? NO, never. Babe I swear."

"Don't fucking call me babe! So, were you ever going to tell me?" he asks.

"Babe...I mean Demetrius. It never even crossed my mind. I swear. It had been so long since we had been together like that and

I had fallen in love with you. I honestly didn't even give it a second thought."

"Yeah right. You guys were trying to set me up the whole time."

"Set you up? How? For what?" she asks.

"Those mutha fuckers are going down, trust me when I say that, and I hope you fucking go with them!"

He slams the front door so hard Janessa can feel the ground unsettle beneath her. Her body numb, she stares at the spot Demetrius last stood. The silence is more piercing than his yelling. Prior to meeting Demetrius, she thought she felt all-alone in the world but that feeling is nothing in comparison to the loneliness she feels now. She feels like she is the only human being on the earth. She wants to cry, but she can't, there's nothing left in the tank for her to even cry. Her breathing slows as she starts to feel her limbs again. She lifts herself off the couch and glides into the kitchen toward the knife block. She grabs the largest knife and gently lifts it out of the holder.

Sun light from the bay window flickers off the point of the knife and she watches the light bounce around the kitchen cabinets. The light bounces around playfully and freely and Janessa begins to reminisce about a summer in her childhood when almost every day she, her sister and cousins would drag out the slip and slide and spend the whole day sliding up and down the long blue piece of plastic. She smiles to herself remembering a time when her life was carefree and she was happy. Her grip on the knife tightens and her pink and white nails dig into her skin. Janessa takes a deep breath, closes her eyes and raises the knife in the air.

TWELVE

A bruptly she feels a strong force grab her wrist so hard that she screeches in the pain. The knife falls to the floor making such a ruckus that the dogs come charging to her rescue. Janessa hasn't opened her eyes yet but she can hear the dogs barking and whimpering. The mysterious force moves to her waist and she is lifted off her feet and carried to the family room where she is plopped on the couch.

"What were you about to do!?"

Janessa still has no idea who is speaking to her.

"Janessa, Janessa, Wake up dammit!"

She finally distinguishes Vick's voice.

"Vick?" she gurgles.

"Yes. What were you going to do? Was this because of me?" he asks.

"No." Janessa says at last opening her eyes.

Vick sits down next to Janessa on the couch, sweating and panting like an overheated dog.

"How did you get in here?" she asks.

"I came to check on you and the front door was unlocked. I called out for you and when I came in the kitchen that's when I saw…" his voice fades.

"I don't know." whispers Janessa.

"You don't know what?"

"You asked me what I was going to do. My answer is I don't know."

The thickness in the air makes Janessa begin to cough. Vick gets up and grabs her a glass of water. She struggles to sip the water in between coughs.

"Was this because of me?" asks Vick somberly.

"No and yes." responds Janessa.

"That is why I originally came over here. To apologize again. You have to know I would have never…you know…I wouldn't have done that to you."

Janessa looks away and closes her eyes trying to stop the tears from falling but she fails. The tears begin to fall in rapid succession.

"I've lost everything." she says.

"You and me both." says Vick.

"You couldn't have lost more than me."

"How would you know how much I have lost? This is not the life I wanted. I got sucked into this thing just like you did."

"I was blackmailed. You did it because you were mad with the police department. There is a big difference." she snaps.

"You only know half the story, trust me."

"So what? I really can't begin to care about anybody else's problems but my own." she says.

"Fair enough. So are you going to sit around and sulk or are you going to make moves and get the fuck out."

Janessa stares across the room pondering his question. Using her t-shirt to wipe tears from her eyes she gets up from the couch and stands in front of the large windows in the family room.

"So?" asks Vick.

She continues to stare out of the window. She watches the squirrels play a game of tag in the yard.

"So I'm going to do something. Something drastic as it appears that is the only way I will be free from you two."

"Hey if it were up to me, you would have been free a long time ago."

" I'm feeling much better now. You can leave. Thanks for stopping by though," she says coldly.

"Damn. Okay then. You're welcome." says Vick.

He swiftly leaves the home. Janessa makes her way to her bedroom to take a shower. As the hot steam from the multiple shower heads begin to engulf her body she slowly inhales then exhales the hot steam. Once out of the shower she can hear the special ringtone set for her sister Angel. She runs to answer the phone almost slipping on the heated tile. She answers right before her sister hangs up.

"Hey girl how's it going?" asks Angel.

"Well not so good." replies Janessa.

Janessa is prepared to tell Angel everything, but just as she is about to spill her guts the phone goes dead.

"Hello, hello, Angel? Hello?" says Janessa.

Janessa looks at the phone. It says call lost. She tries to dial her sister back but it beeps busy. Janessa figures Angel must be trying to call her back as well so she waits a few seconds for her phone to ring, but it doesn't. She tries to dial her again, but again she gets a busy signal. Frustrated Janessa lobs the phone across the room and watches it shatter into small pieces as it hits the floor. She tip-toes over to the area where pieces of her diamond studded phone case lay about the floor. Janessa admires how something damaged and broken can still look beautiful under the right circumstances.

She gets herself together and leaves the house to buy a new cell phone. She is about to pull off when Demetrius black pickup truck screeches into her driveway and blocks her in. Her lips press together in a slight grimace. She has no energy to argue with him or offer more apologies. Demetrius exits the truck, flexing his arm muscles and walks over to the passenger side window of Janessa's Porsche Cayenne SUV. He attempts to open the door but Janessa locks it.

"Really? You're not going to let me in?" grumbles Demetrius.

"What do you want?" Janessa screams through the window.

"I want to talk. Open the door!"

Janessa doesn't open the door, but rolls down the passenger window half way.

"So that's how you want to play it huh?" asks Demetrius.

"I'm tired. I can't fight with you right now."

"I didn't come here to fight."

"I couldn't tell from the way you drove in here."

"I'm sorry about that. I can't help but be upset that the woman I love, slept with my enemy." says Demetrius.

Janessa blushes a little and unlocks the door. Demetrius gets in the SUV.

"Where are you headed?" he asks.

"To get a new cell phone."

"I'll go with you and we can talk on the way."

"Sure. Can you move your truck please?"

"Oh yeah. My bad. How about I just drive." says Demetrius.

"That's fine."

The two get out of her SUV and into his pickup truck.

"So what's wrong with your cell phone?"

"Dropped it and the screen cracked."

"Damn. That sucks. At least you have the money to buy a new one right."

"I guess." says Janessa.

"I came back because even though I am hurt and upset. I shouldn't have said the things I said and I shouldn't have left like that."

"All I can say is I'm sorry. I don't know what else to do or say." responds Janessa.

"I know. Look I can't say I'm completely over it. Either way I want you to know that I'm still here for you and I'm still going to help you break free from them."

Janessa's empty eyes look back at him.

"Janessa did you hear me? I'm still going to help you."

"No." she says.

"No! No what?" asks Demetrius.

"No. I don't want you to help me. I'm going to break free of them myself."

"Oh yeah. How you do you suppose you're going to do that?" asks Demetrius.

"I'm going to walk away."

Laughter fills the truck. The truck swerves out of the lane as Demetrius continues to uncontrollably laugh at Janessa's statement. Janessa holds on to her door handle as she waits for Demetrius to get control of the truck.

"Really? You believe it will be that easy. I've seen them kill people for less."

"You've personally seen them kill people?"

"Well maybe not personally. But I know they are cold-blooded killers and they have killed people for things like bringing the wrong change."

"Vick?" she asks.

"Vick what?"

"Vick kills or has killed people?"

"Why do you think he was kicked out of the department. They learned he was a complete psychopath , killing suspects and then trying to make it look like a justified shooting. He even strangled a guy to death and got away with it."

Bile shoots up into Janessa's throat. She swallows the bitter liquid back down and lays her head on the window.

"Yep that's right. You were sleeping with a psychotic killer." Demetrius says with glee.

"I thought the police department railroaded him and framed him to look like the bad guy."

"Wow, he really had you fooled. Did you love him or something?" "At one point I thought I did." Janessa cringes inwardly.

They pull into the parking lot of a small shopping center. Demetrius passes several open spots at the front and parks what seems like miles from the shopping mall.

"What made you change your mind? Me?" he asks.

"No. I realized I didn't love him long before you came into the picture. I was lonely that's all and he filled the void temporarily." she says.

"You know you're lucky they haven't already killed you." Demetrius says coldly.

"What?"

"Trust me. I know them better than you ever will and they get what they need from people and then they dispose of them."

"I guess they still need me then."

"Exactly. That was made clear after your meeting with Malcolm the other day."

"So. I'm safe then. Right?" she asks.

"Yeah I believe so. I'm just not sure how much longer they'll need you. I've heard rumors. Let's go inside and get your new phone."

"No! Not until you explain. What rumors?"

Demetrius cracks his neck to the left. A bad habit Janessa wishes he would stop. He turns the radio up and leans in closer to Janessa.

"Because any minute now your whole operation is going to be struck down by the DEA and they know it."

The blood drains from the top of Janessa's head down to her toes and her hands begin to tremble violently.

"Wh-a-a-t do you mean?" she stutters.

"I mean exactly what I said. Any day now. It's going down and they are making moves as we speak to get the fuck out of dodge before it does."

"What about me!" shrieks Janessa.

"Honestly you're a loose end. That is why everyone was shocked to find out you were still six feet above ground. You see what he did to Nikki. But it's clear why you're still here. You were fucking one of the bad guys."

"Wait...what? Who's everyone? What the fuck is going on Demetrius!" Janessa shouts.

She can feel the blood rushing back up from her toes to her brain in a hot fury. The temperature of her skin rises. . Her lungs quickly expel oxygen and carbon dioxide in and out of her body. Demetrius now cracks the right side of his neck.

"I guess it's time you know the truth. But not here. Let's go get your phone and we'll talk on the way back to your house."

Her chest is still rising and falling at a rapid pace as she tries to process everything that Demetrius just said. Feelings of fear, anxiety, desperation and confusion alternate between themselves as they make the long walk from the truck to the shopping center. The sun beams on her face with a vengeance and she does what she can to block it. The walk to the shopping mall feels like an eternity with the click-clack of her yellow flip-flops sounding louder and louder. Demetrius long strides prevent her from keeping up with him. They make it into the store. Janessa knows exactly what she wants and they're in and out in a matter of twenty minutes with Janessa's new phone. The walk back to the truck doesn't feel as long; they are both distracted. Demetrius talks on his phone the whole way and Janessa tinkers with her new phone.

Back in the truck Janessa immediately launches into a line of questions sounding as if she is questioning a witness on direct examination. It's clear that Janessa is not going to relent until she gets some answers so Demetrius decides to pull over onto a side street where he can answer her questions.

"So I was assigned to you." he confesses.

"Assigned to me?"

"Yes. You were my assignment. The DEA has been investigating these guys for months and then suddenly you came into the picture. We couldn't figure out if you were a willing participant or not, so I was assigned the tasks of figuring out what your role was in the business."

"So…" her voice trails off.

"No. It's not what you're thinking. My feelings for you are real. I swear. Undercover work is so complicated and you do all kinds of things you wouldn't normally do, but I developed real feelings for you along the way."

"I can't believe you put on that big show when you found out about Vick and I and all this time…you were the liar!" she booms.

"It wasn't a show. I was hurt and upset because I do care about you. I knew a lot of things before starting this assignment but I never knew that you and Vick had a sexual relationship."

Janessa's notices the side road Demetrius pulled over on is eerily dark and unoccupied. The darkness makes her nervous. Anything could happen to her out here and nobody would know.

"So what's going to happen to me?" she asks.

"You're going to have to go into witness protection while they await trial and then you're going to need to testify."

"And after I testify?"

"Unfortunately even if they go to jail forever you would remain in witness protection for a long time."

"What's a long time?"

"At least ten years."

"Ten years! Why?"

"They are powerful even in prison and if they want you dead, which they will, they can still make it happen from prison." Demetrius avows.

"How did this become my life?" asks Janessa to herself. Demetrius doesn't know the answer to that question, turns the truck back on and drives to Janessa's home. When they pull into the driveway her eyes are glossy. She realizes that she will never actually be rid of her blackmailers and they will forever control her life. She has nobody to blame but herself. She had choices and she chose to steal the money from Malcolm and she chose to work for them to cover her own ass. She chose to enjoy the money and spend it. They sit mutely in the winding driveway.

"Don't look at it as bad news. It's good news. Really." he mutters.

"I need to rest. Will I know when it is all going down?"

"No. Even I don't know that. It will be hard but you're going to have to continue working for them like nothing is amiss."

"I think I've mastered the art of lying to myself and others. I'll be fine. Goodnight."

She jumps out of the truck and goes into her house.

THIRTEEN

The next morning, she decides to forgo the R & R Malcolm offered her and go into the office. She has nothing to do with her free time, now that she and Demetrius are in an awkward place. It is business as usual. Janessa goes to work like nothing is different. She tries to forget the fight with Demetrius, the visit from Vick, the assault from Vick and finally the conversation with Demetrius. She pushes the memories all down, tucked away in a part of her brain where it can't be retrieved. She is numb and it feels good. No worries, no cares, no stress. She goes through the motions of serving clients and making money. She hears nothing from Malcolm and Vick all day and the only person she has contact with is Big Mike. Big Mike is on his usual guard duties and at the end of the day he walks Janessa to her car.

"You okay? You seemed pretty out of it today?" Big Mike asks Janessa.

"I don't know.. I think I should have taken that R & R Malcolm offered and taken a vacation." she responds.

"It's coming soon." he says.

"What?" asks Janessa.

"Oh um I meant you're right. You should have taken him up on his offer and taken off somewhere. You certainly have the money to do so."

Janessa's eyes bore in Big Mike.

"That's not what you meant." she contests.

"It's been a long day and the words just came out wrong."

"Sure."

She peers at him one more time and gets into her BMW. As soon as she starts the car she calls Vick on her cell phone using the hands free through her car radio. It rings and rings. Each ring Janessa gets more and more frustrated. Right before she is about to end the call he answers.

"Hello." Vick answers.

"Where have you been?" asks Janessa.

"Um at home. Why? Something go down at the firm today?"

"No. Everything was business as usual."

"Okay. You didn't need me then. Plus, Big Mike was there right?"

"Yes, but since when did you stop checking in?"

"I didn't always check in. That was Malcolm's thing always paranoid something would go wrong if he didn't have some kind of oversight." Vick maintains.

"But I didn't hear from him either."

"Oh really? I haven't heard from him today myself."

"Is that weird? You know, for you not to hear from him?" she asks.

"Yes and no. I mean I'm not his babysitter. He can do as he pleases, but I generally hear something from him daily. Even if it's just some random story about some bitch he just fucked." he says.

"So what do you suppose is going on?" asks Janessa.

"Probably nothing. I'm sure when you go to work tomorrow he will be in the office getting the cash out of the safe."

"Oh. So... I have nothing to worry about then."

"Nope." stresses Vick.

"Well okay then."

"Okay. Talk to you later."

Vick's explanation seemed plausible, but Janessa doesn't feel good. The memories she fought to push away are rising to the surface again. She is remembering what Demetrius said about their willingness to kill anybody they didn't need any more. If they know they are being investigated then why wouldn't they take all the money, kill her and make a run for it. She is nothing but a liability to them now. But of course, Demetrius would never let that happen. Would he? Her head is spinning as she drives home. She decides she can't be alone tonight and makes a B-line to her sister Angel's house. Now, ultra-paranoid she feels like every black car or truck that trails behind her is following her. She can't risk putting her family in harm's way so she makes her way to a Holiday Inn in downtown Baltimore instead.

Her nerves are wreaking havoc on her head and stomach. As people trickle into the lobby of the hotel Janessa observes how happy and carefree they appear to be and she wishes she could have those feelings again. She purchases both Tums and Advil at the hotel gift shop and makes her way to her room. Ring, ring, ring... blares her phone. It's her sister, Angel. She misses her sister, her family, her life prior to ever meeting Vick and Malcolm. Janessa answers the phone and again she gets a scolding about not contacting her or anybody else in the family. And once again all Janessa can do is apologize for her neglect. She has run out of excuses and explanations and thus doesn't try to give either to her worried sister. She allows her sister to scold her for another fifteen minutes before she finally rushes her off the phone on the premise that she had to get to some work done.

The room is soft and innocent; everything Janessa's life is not. The white fluffy comforter, big fluffy white pillows and the large heavy, white curtains hanging from the windows leads Janessa to envision that this is what heaven must look like. She falls back onto the king size bed and quickly falls asleep. Morning sunrays fall upon her face gently waking her up. She slept through everything including several phone calls . Her phones blue LED blinks alerting Janessa to numerous missed calls, voicemails and text messages. No surprise that all of them are from either Malcolm, Vick or Demetrius. She realizes how much this trio of men completely dictate every move she makes in her life. Janessa doesn't read the messages or listen to the voicemails right away. Instead she makes some coffee and watches the morning news. She begins to gasp for air at the shock of what she is seeing on the local news.

Breaking News, Breaking News scrolls across the top of her flat screen television. Notorious drug dealer Malcolm Jacobs arrested at his mansion in Annapolis, Maryland. After stabilizing herself from chocking on the coffee she hurries to her phone to check the text messages and voicemails. Demetrius voicemail is first and it's barely audible. She is certain that he says "we got him", "we got him" over and over. Then she checks her text messages from Vick that reads: Get the fuck out of town now! Then, finally Malcolm's voicemail which oddly enough is the only calm message of the bunch. He states he hasn't spoken to Janessa in a couple of days and he would like to meet with her to discuss some business. His message came it at 12:56 a.m., Demetrius voicemail came exactly an hour later at 1:56 a.m., and Vicks text message came in at 1:58a.m.

Her eyes sparkle and gleam as she jumps up and down on the bed. It's finally over. She's free! She begins to yell at the top of her lungs. "I'm free, I'm free. Thank you, Jesus. I'm free!!" She is so loud that a staff member from the hotel comes to her room to check on her. She ensures him she is doing just fine and apologizes if she startled any of the other guests. Janessa is prancing around the room with joy when she begins to think about Vick and that he must have gotten away somehow, which means he is still free to hurt Janessa if he so desired. But he tried to warn her per the text message so why would he want to hurt her?

She remembers Demetrius warning about the dangerousness and viciousness of the two men. She is a witness, of course he would want to hurt her. Her joy quickly turns to fear. She picks her phone off the bed to call Demetrius; however, before she can dial there is a booming knock at her hotel door.

"I'm busy. Come back later please." says Janessa through the door.

"BOOM, BOOM, BOOM!"

"I said I'm busy. No housekeeping right now!" she hollers.

"Open this fucking door or I'll shoot the door knob off!" yells a familiar voice.

It's Vick!

"Vick?"

"You know damn well it's me. Open the fucking door."

She hesitates but opens it as she knows she has no real choice.

He pushes past her knocking her to the floor.

"Where the fuck is he?" he roars.

"Who?"

"Don't play games with me. Your lames ass cop boyfriend, that's who!"

"He's not here. I checked in by myself, I swear."

Vick turns to the television just in time to hear the news anchor reporting on Malcolm's arrest. He grabs the remote and turns the volume up to the maximum volume. "At around 1:00 a.m. this morning, notorious and violent drug dealer Malcolm Jacobs was arrested on an arrest warrant by the Baltimore DEA field office with the assistance of the Anne Arundel County Sheriff's Office at his luxury home in Annapolis, Maryland." The police report that the arrest went without incident and Mr. Jacobs is now sitting in an Annapolis County jail, waiting for transport to federal lock up. The U.S. Attorney appears on the screen and begins to speak.

"Mr. Jacobs is a person of interest in several murders, drug trafficking and drug distribution investigations and we are happy to report that he is now off the streets and in custody. He may have escaped justice in the past, but we firmly believe that we have all we need to put him away for good."

Vick turns off the television, but then continues to stare at it as if it were still on. Janessa remains on the floor, afraid to move. She scoots on her butt toward the bed so she can use it to support her back. He continues to stare at the blank television screen. Where is Demetrius she wonders. He finally breaks from his trance.

"So did you get my text message?" he asks calmly.

"Your text message?"

"Yes. This morning. Telling you to get out of town."

"Oh um yes. When I woke up." she says.

"Well…" he says.

"Well I will if that is what you think I should do." she says.

"Do you want to live?" he asks.

"Of course." Janessa declares.

"I should end this for you right now."

She sits frozen to the floor. The blood in her veins turn ice cold and she begins to shiver.

"But I won't."

And just like that Vick coolly darts out of the room. Janessa remains frozen. In her mind, she can see herself rushing out of the room to the bank to withdraw as much money as she can and jetting out of town. But she can't get her body to react. She is frozen in place. Janessa begins to breath quickly in the hopes that her blood will finally warm and she will be able to get up. It seems like hours later as opposed to minutes but she is at last able to rise and stagger from the room. She quickly checks out and speeds home. She is both relieved and surprised that cops and SWAT are not surrounding her beautiful home.

As she runs into the house and begins to throw random clothing items into her large designer suitcase, she notices that Truth and Justice didn't greet her at the door.

"Truth? Justice?" she yells from her bedroom. "Hey guys… where are you? Come to mommy."

Nothing. She creeps through the long hallways of the home cautiously peeking her head into each room calling for her dogs.

But they are nowhere to be found. Then a frightening idea comes to her. What if Vick hurt them? Would he do something like that? Yes, he could and he would. She begins to sob as she continues to check each individual room for her babies.

"Truth, Justice" her voice quivers through the tears. She is at least relieved not to find their dead bodies somewhere. She doesn't have much time left to get out of town so she grabs a few more things and takes off out the back door. She drags her suitcase around the corner to her to BMW. She is about to put her foot to the medal when someone bangs on her driver side window. She jerks back and the hair on her arms stand up. It's Demetrius.

"Thank God!" gushes Janessa.

"Baby! We did it! We did it!" declares Demetrius.

Janessa leaps out of the car and hugs Demetrius tightly around his neck.

"Is it really over?" Janessa asks still holding on tight to Demetrius.

"Yes baby. It's really over." He says as he squeezes her waist.

The two continue to embrace as Janessa does something she hasn't been able to do in a long time. She breathes a sigh of relief. Demetrius explains to her that she is safe and she doesn't have to leave town. They have apprehended Vick too and it is truly over. Even more, he has secured her babies Truth and Justice with the dog sitter. As Demetrius explains how it all went down Janessa feels like she is in a dream. She can't believe it's happened. She can go back to normal life, no more selling drugs, no more dealing with the crazy antics of Malcolm and Vick. She can be with her family again. All she must do is testify against Malcolm and Vick, which she is happy to oblige.

Eight months have passed and Janessa is still waiting to testify against Malcolm and Vick. She declined witness protection, as she can no longer fathom the idea of living in the shadows anymore. She wanted to be with her family again. She wanted to feel normal again. And with Demetrius by her side she felt safe. The DEA and FBI don't truly believe she was a total unwilling participant in the drug dealing business, but they need her to be part of the United States case so she was promised immunity from prosecution. Even so, she hated the fact that she is still waiting for the signed paperwork from the U.S. Attorney's Office verifying their promise not to prosecute. Demetrius and her lawyer continue to assure her that it is just a matter of time, so she has no real worries. Life is good.

It's a cloudy Thursday morning. Janessa wakes up in her modest two-bedroom apartment. The government required that she give up all the assets she gained while working with Malcolm and Vick. That included the cars, jewelry, homes, paintings, etc. She didn't mind. None of it was worth the stress she endured. The stress of it all caused her to lose way too much weight and she was practically bald from all the hair loss! She has taken a job as a courtroom clerk. She wanted to be close to the legal profession, despite being suspended from the Maryland Bar for a year. As she gets dressed for work an ominous feeling trails her around the apartment. She chalks it up to her being upset about the fight she and Demetrius had last night.

Lately he has been unusually edgy and moody which has led to a lot of fights. Janessa felt like he was doing it on purpose, like he was trying to distance himself from her by picking fights. At work, she tries her best to shake the feeling of doom but it won't go away. Then she sees a familiar face approaching her. It's Agent Rodgers, one of the DEA agents that first interviewed her after Malcolm and Vick were arrested. Her mouth turns upward when she sees him and she gives him a wave, but he doesn't wave or smile back at her. As he continues to approach her everything slows down. Before she can even say good morning, he is putting her hands behind her back and slapping handcuffs on her!

The sound of metal clanking rings in her ears. Janessa hears Agent Rodgers speak but she can't understand the words. As life fades from her pretty brown eyes, disbelief and confusion consume her. Members of the bar, litigants, and judge's watch in shock as she is ushered out of the Baltimore City courtroom in handcuffs. She makes the hike down the long, marble courtroom floors. Beady eyes peer at her. She keeps her head down and focuses on Agent Rodgers shiny black shoes for direction. Just as she is being helped into the dark sedan she observes a heavily tinted white SUV across the street. A window begins to come down and to Janessa's alarm Nikki's face peeks out the back seat of the driver side and she is smiling from ear to ear.

Her mouth falls open, and with a rise in her voice she bellows at Agent Rodgers as he tries to get her into the idling car.

"Wait, wait, wait!"

Then the driver side window slowly rolls down but only half way. There is a shadow over their face and Janessa can merely see the person from the nose up, but she doesn't need to see anymore to know exactly who it is.

"No, no!" she screams.

"Janessa you need to get into the car right now!" scowls Agent Rodgers.

"But, but...I don't understand...what is happening?" she asks.

"It's really in your best interest not to speak right now. As I advised before and as you surely know being a former attorney you should exercise your right to remain silent."

Janessa calms down.

"You're right Agent. You're certainly right."

She sits in the car as instructed and she and Agent Rodgers drive right past the SUV. As they pass the occupants in the SUV, Janessa straightens up and with composure parts her lips and mouths one word. REVENGE.

THE BEGINNING....

Made in the USA
Las Vegas, NV
24 May 2021

23579108R20100